ADDITIONAL PRAISE FOR
THE REX GRAVES MYSTERY SERIES

Murder Comes Calling

"Satisfying … Smooth prose will keep cozy fans turning the pages."

—*Publishers Weekly*

"Nicely mixes procedural detail and village charm and will appeal to fans of Deborah Crombie and Anne Cleeland."

—*Booklist*

Murder at Midnight

"A classic country-house mystery, with modern day twists and turns adding to the fun."

—*Booklist*

"What could be better for Agatha Christie whodunit fans than an old-fashioned, Scottish country house murder on New Year's Eve? "

—*Mystery Scene*

"*Murder at Midnight* will delight all cozy and Agatha Christie fans. C. S. creates devilishly complex characters, keeping the reader on edge until the final page … C. S.'s best work to date."

—*Suspense Magazine*

Murder of the Bride

"This is a well-crafted read and a logical and well-plotted conclusion."

—*Crime Fiction Lovers*

Murder on the Moor

"C. S. Challinor delivers a racier cozy in *Murder on the Moor* … skillfully choreographed."

—*Washington Post*

"Conten   voice, it'll have you
guessing

—*RT Book Reviews*

"A welcome diversion from today's style of writing... The writing is crisp and the story fast-paced. Challinor doesn't waste time on empty filler, but gets right to the topic at hand."

—*BellaOnline*

Phi Beta Murder

"This is a well-paced mystery that plays fair with the reader and provides a satisfying and surprising conclusion. The writing is crisp and dialogue-driven."

—*Mystery Scene*

"Humor and well-written characters add to the story, as does some reflection on the causes of suicide. A wonderful read and great plot for cozy mystery lovers."

—*ForeWord Reviews*

Murder in the Raw

"*Murder in the Raw* is a clever variant on the locked room mystery. With a host of colorful characters, a dose of humor, and a balmy locale, you will want to devour this well-plotted mystery."

—*Mystery Scene*

"A solid choice for traditional mystery fans, *Murder in the Raw* provides some new twists on something old and familiar."

—*Mystery Reader*

"*Murder in the Raw* is one of the more recent contributions to a growing library of mystery novels of interest to naturists, and naked readers will especially enjoy how Challinor 'gets it right.'"

—*N: Nude and Natural*

Christmas is Murder

*"[A] winner... At times, it seems we are playing Clue or perhaps enjoying a contemporary retelling of a classic Agatha Christie tale (*And Then There Were None*, or *At Bertram's Hotel*) with a charming new sleuth. A must for cozy fans."

—*Booklist* (starred review)

"Challinor's debut is a pleasant modern knockoff of Christie."

—*Kirkus Reviews*

"Graves's next case may be worth watching for."

—*Ellery Queen Mystery Magazine*

"Challinor will keep most readers guessing as she cleverly spreads suspicion and clues that point in one direction, then another."

—*Alfred Hitchcock Mystery Magazine*

"A great start to a new series that is sure to become a modern favorite traditional English cozy series."

—*The Mystery Reader*

"Agatha Christie fans, here you go! You have been waiting for a mystery writer that can hold the torch; well, we found her: C. S. Challinor."

—*Suspense Magazine*

"*Christmas is Murder* is a most enjoyable first mystery in what promises to be a fantastic series. Challinor writes with wit and cheek, and with Rex Graves she has created a thoroughly charming sleuth."

—Rick Miller, host of ABC's
primetime hit series *Just for Laughs*

"C. S. Challinor has crafted a delectable murder mystery set in an old English manor turned hotel. Christmas is Murder has all the charm and ambience of a classic Agatha Christie novel. This is mystery at its very best! Challinor is an author to watch. I'll be anxiously awaiting her next book!"

—Nancy Mehl, author of The Ivy Towers Mystery Series

UPSTAGED
— BY —
MURDER

A Rex Graves Mystery

UPSTAGED
— BY —
MURDER

C. S. CHALLINOR

MIDNIGHT INK
WOODBURY, MINNESOTA

FIRST EDITION
First Printing, 2018

Book format by Cassie Willett
Cover design by Kevin R. Brown
Cover art © Dominick Finelle / The July Group

Midnight Ink, an imprint of Llewellyn Worldwide Ltd.

This is a work of fiction. Names, characters, places, and incidents are either the product of the author's imagination or are used fictitiously, and any resemblance to actual persons living or dead, business establishments, events, or locales is entirely coincidental.

Library of Congress Cataloging-in-Publication Data
Names: Challinor, C. S. (Caroline S.), author.
Title: Upstaged by murder : a Rex Graves mystery / C. S. Challinor.
Description: Woodbury, Minnesota : Midnight Ink, [2018] | Series: Rex Graves
  ; [9] | Description based on print version record and CIP data provided by
  publisher; resource not viewed.
Identifiers: LCCN 2018004409 (print) | LCCN 2018006099 (ebook) | ISBN
  9780738756684 | ISBN 9780738756479 (softcover : acid-free paper)
Subjects: LCSH: Graves, Rex (Fictitious character)—Fiction. |
  Lawyers—Scotland—Fiction. | Murder—Investigation—Fiction. | Private
  investigators—Fiction. | GSAFD: Mystery fiction. | Legal stories.
Classification: LCC PS3603.H3366 (ebook) | LCC PS3603.H3366 U67 2018
(print)
  | DDC 813/.6—dc23
LC record available at https://lccn.loc.gov/2018004409

Midnight Ink
Llewellyn Worldwide Ltd.
2143 Wooddale Drive
Woodbury, MN 55125-2989
www.midnightinkbooks.com

Printed in the United States of America

For readers of murder mysteries everywhere;
each and every one. Without you, writing them
would become, quite literally, a dying art.

CAST OF CHARACTERS

Peril At Pinegrove Hall

——————— A Play ———————

Written by Penny Spencer

Lady Naomi Grove—Cassie Chase
Clara Grove—Susan Richardson
Henry Chalmers—Trey Atkins
Robin Busket—Bobbi Shaw
Mr. Farley—Paul Reddit
Miss Marple—Ada Card
Hercule Poirot—Dennis Caldwell
Lord Peter Wimsey—Andrew Forsythe
Sherlock Holmes—Rodney Snyder
Father Brown—Timothy Holden
Dorkins—Christopher Ells

ONE

A SENSE OF ANTICIPATION filled the hall on this opening night of the play, accompanied by excited chatter and preemptory clearings of the throat. Rex Graves sat with his new wife in the front row facing a stage draped with ruby red curtains falling to the floor in heavy folds of velvet. He shifted position on the uncomfortable folding chair, envious of those spectators with the foresight to bring cushions, presumably regular community theatre-goers who had learnt the hard way.

"How long is the play?" he asked Helen, applying a light tone to his educated Scots burr, not wishing to convey his physical discomfort, lest she think he was complaining.

"A couple of hours, I imagine. I really think you'll enjoy it. It's a whodunit—right up your street." She wore a dress in blue jersey that clung to her generous curves, her blonde hair twisted up and held in place by an ornamental clasp. "It makes a pleasant change from going to the cinema."

"The cinema has plusher seating. You look scrumptious, by the way."

From the row behind, a querulous female voice muttered, "I won't be able to see around this big man."

Rex sank lower in his chair, rounding his shoulders in an attempt to reduce his bulk, and leafed through the programme that had been handed out at the main entrance listing the cast and actors' bios. Entitled *Peril at Pinegrove Hall,* the play included five famous sleuths from bygone eras and the usual pool of suspects found in a manor house mystery. Reflecting that the title did not bode well for the actors nor, he feared, for the audience, he placed the leaflet on the scuffed parquet floor beneath his chair with a resigned sigh and, resuming his awkward posture, fantasised about a cold Guinness and a long soak in the bath.

His back felt stiff from the long drive from Edinburgh that morning, and even though there was plenty of legroom in the front row, he dared not stretch his out while people were still finding their seats. Suddenly, the overhead lights dimmed and a hush fell over the hall.

The curtains parted to reveal a parlour scene of overstuffed velour sofas and armchairs arranged around a large Persian rug. Much of the furniture was occupied by figures in shadow, but as the stage lights brightened, the actors and props gradually took on colour and contour. A few spectators clapped.

"It is very curious, I think," pronounced a foreign-accented individual mincing across the stage in a three-piece pinstripe suit and sprats, his gleaming hair and waxed moustache unnaturally dark.

Rex fancied he could almost smell the pomade. A murmur of recognition rose from the audience.

"Dashed curious," agreed a taller man in morning dress, lounging by a fireplace to the left of the stage. He screwed a monocle into his eye socket to better examine a gilt-framed portrait that hung above the mantelpiece.

"All the more curious for me," riposted a man seated in an armchair and holding a meerschaum pipe; a deerstalker cap perched on his knee. "It seems I precede you all, chronologically speaking."

"Indeed, your reputation precedes you, my dear Holmes," said the man by the fireplace, removing his monocle and bestowing a bow. "The rest of us merely follow in your disquisitive example."

Why not just say investigative? Rex asked himself.

"I'm delighted to be included in such illustrious company," tinkled a voice in the far-right corner, where a white-haired lady in a blue silk frock sat placidly knitting on a Chesterfield. Behind the sofa loomed a folding Chinese screen, a plumed fern in a bronze urn beside it adding a touch of greenery to the set.

"Will this take long, I wonder?" A stumpy village priest in a long, black, buttoned coat and white collar stood looking out a painted window, a large round hat in his hand. "I left Flambeau fishing at the lake and now it is pouring down," he lamented.

The elderly woman lowered her knitting. "I expect Lady Naomi Grove and her solicitor are hoping the five of us can put our heads together and solve this most perplexing mystery with all speed."

"Well, where in deuce *are* our hosts?" enquired Sherlock. "I need to get back to London by three to meet with Watson."

"They are doubtless waiting for us to assemble and become acquainted, and then we shall surely hear more about why we, of all the detectives in England, were invited to Pinegrove Hall. Two purl, three plain," the knitter counted as she took up her needles again.

"But the answer to that is most clear," replied Poirot. "We are the *crème de la crème*, are we not?" And, cocking an ear: "Ah, I believe I hear steps in the *foyer*."

The solid French doors at the back of the parlour opened on cue and a lugubrious butler in black coattails and white gloves announced, "Lady Naomi Grove and Miss Robin Busket, if you please."

A willowy redhead made her entrance in a wide-shouldered blouse and narrow mid-length skirt, followed by a more robust female wearing a tweed jacket, jodhpurs, and riding boots.

"Apologies for keeping you all waiting," Lady Naomi declared, motioning to Mr. Holmes to remain seated and moving towards the front of the stage. She turned to the butler. "Dorkins, see to it that tea is brought in for ten people. My aunt and Mr. Farley will be joining us. And Henry Chalmers," she added with a tender smile, gazing out to the audience in loving reflection, her hair, falling in loose waves to her shoulders, shining a reddish gold under the lights. The butler left.

"Robin," she said, addressing the woman in jodhpurs. "Let me introduce you, in no particular order, to: Miss Jane Marple."

The spinster beamed from the Chesterfield.

"Father Brown."

The bespectacled clergyman stumbled forward and murmured a greeting.

"Lord Peter Wimsey."

His lordship bowed most gallantly.

"Sherlock Holmes."

The gentleman detective, who had stood despite Lady Naomi's entreaty to remain seated, inclined his head politely.

"And Monsieur Hercule Poirot himself."

"Ah, *mademoiselle*, you do me a great honour." The diminutive Belgian sleuth took her hand and, inclining his egg-shaped head, kissed it with effusive Gallic courtesy.

"Miss Robin Busket here is my aunt's companion," Lady Naomi said, wrapping up the introductions. "Now, I'm sure you are all wondering why you were called to Pinegrove Hall at such short notice, and I am so very glad you *were* able to attend. As indicated in the invitation, a handsome reward is being offered for the recovery of a priceless heirloom that went missing from this house the night before last."

"*Mademoiselle*," remonstrated Poirot obsequiously, planting himself in the middle of the rug and twiddling his upturned moustache. "Perhaps I may speak for all when I say we are not motivated by reward but by renown!"

"I could not've put it better myself," said the debonair Peter Wimsey. "And may the best man—or lady," he added with a small bow to Miss Marple, "win!"

"Well, I, for one, should like to know more about this intriguing little competition before I can agree to participate," countered Holmes with a haughty sneer. "An urgent matter awaits me in the city." He sat back down and, crossing his legs, took a puff on his pipe.

The French doors opened and three more people entered. Striding to Lady Naomi's side, an elegant young man clasped her hands to his chest.

"This is Henry Chalmers. We are newly engaged to be married," the hostess declared.

A flurry of congratulations circulated the parlour.

"Aunt Clara," she said, wrenching her gaze from the young man's face and addressing the female newcomer, an older woman dressed severely in black. "As you can see, our guests are all here."

The equestrian Robin Busket stepped towards the aunt. "Clara, dear, come and sit by the fire. You look chilled to the bone." The frail woman let her companion guide her to a sofa.

Lady Naomi gestured towards the middle-aged man in a dark suit who had come in with Henry Chalmers and Aunt Clara. "Mr. Farley is our family solicitor and a dear friend. We may now proceed."

The solicitor commenced by clearing his throat. "A bejewelled gold goblet belonging to the family since the French Revolution has been stolen and must be restored forthwith," he explained to the detectives in well-modulated tones, while Lady Naomi and her fiancé joined hands and stood back a few paces. "A parlour maid noticed its disappearance from this very room first thing yesterday. No guests have been staying at Pinegrove Hall in the past week and all exterior doors are locked at night. You will have seen when you drove up that the residence stands amid acres of parkland. The gardeners, gamekeepers, and stable hands left for the annual fair in Middleton three days ago and are due to return tomorrow. That leaves the parlour maid, cook, butler..."

"It's never the butler," Helen whispered in an aside to Rex, just as his attention began to wander.

He glanced along the front row to where Penny Spencer, who had written the play, sat bolt upright in her seat, no doubt praying no one would forget or fudge their lines. So far, the audience seemed enrapt.

At this point, Miss Marple was suggesting the detectives take a look in the attic, in case the thief had hidden up there while waiting for night time, when he could perpetrate the crime undetected.

"In the attic?" repeated Aunt Clara tremulously, clutching a frothy white handkerchief to her throat.

"Well, it's a possibility, isn't it?" Miss Marple chirped. "Unless one of the servants took the goblet, it must be a stranger who would prefer to remain unseen."

"With all due respect, we should not exclude the rest of the household," Sherlock Holmes put in stiffly. Sitting back in his chair, pipe in hand, he pointedly surveyed the aunt's attentive companion, along with the beau, who had been preening in an oval wall mirror and adjusting his floppy cravat.

"I say," Lord Peter Wimsey asked the solicitor, "is the begemmed artefact insured?"

"Indeed it is, but for a fraction of its true value."

"And it belongs to Lady Naomi Grove?"

Mr. Farley gave a brisk nod and indicated the portrait above the fireplace. "The whole estate was bequeathed to Her Ladyship by the late Marquis de Bosquet of Pinegrove Hall. Clara Grove, her paternal aunt, is her only surviving relative."

Rex, huddled on his chair, suppressed a yawn.

"And yet there were rumours of an indiscretion long ago," the solicitor confided in an undertone directed at the audience.

The French doors opened. "Tea is served," intoned the butler bearing a tray laden with silver, which he deposited on a round table centre-stage. "And Mr. Chalmers is wanted on the telephone," he added self-importantly.

"Excuse me, my angel!" The young man exited in a hurry, blowing a kiss to his betrothed.

"I have to wonder..." murmured Robin Busket, gaping after him.

"Henry would never commit such a frightful act," Lady Naomi declared. "In any case, everything I own will become jointly his on the day we wed. Henry loves me for me!"

"I daresay he does, but he has nothing to his name. And I have heard—"

"Lies!" Naomi interjected. "Now, let us get to the bottom of this wretched business without further ado. I shall look in the attic myself!"

"Take one of the gentlemen with you," Aunt Clara pleaded, fluttering the lacy handkerchief in the sleuths' direction.

"No, let them enjoy their tea. There won't be anyone up there now, but I may find a clue."

"Dusty, cobwebby attics are good places for trapping clues," Miss Marple acknowledged. "And, who knows? Perhaps you will find the missing goblet. Alas, I am too old to go exploring with you, and none of our fine gentleman are dressed for it. Poor Father Brown would risk tripping up in his cassock!"

"No matter," said Lady Naomi, waving these objections aside. "I shall go by myself, I tell you."

Helen leaned over to Rex. "Here we go," she whispered. "The Idiot in the Attic scene."

"Shush!" someone hissed from behind.

Helen made big eyes at Rex, who twitched his lips in amusement.

"Naomi, you always were such a headstrong girl," the aunt chided ineffectually. "Pray go with her, Robin."

"I wouldn't hesitate under normal circumstances, as well you know, my dear, but my ankle is still swollen from the fall. Star is such a spirited stallion," she informed the guests. "Naomi, at the very least take your father's revolver with you …"

At this point Rex nodded off, and some minutes later awoke with a start and a soft grunt. A grey screen had materialized onstage, concealing the parlour furniture and replacing it with a shadowy backdrop of old wooden trunks, a broken rocking horse, and a baby carriage. Naomi's head appeared through a trap door in the floor and she looked around cautiously. Presently, the rest of her emerged, a handgun pointed out from her chest. She stood for a moment in an attitude of attentive listening, a spotlight trained on her motionless form. The trap door thudded shut behind her, startling her from her pose.

Utter silence prevailed as the light dimmed, throwing into focus a hand clasping a dagger magnified in silhouette against the grey screen. People in the audience gasped and the curtains began to close upon the scene to a ripple of applause.

As the heavy red panels joined, a blood-chilling scream rang out onstage, followed by a shot. Rex jumped in his chair, as did Helen, whose hand he was holding. The clapping intensified and the lights went back on in the hall.

"What a good ploy!" one spectator in the front row exclaimed. A few turned to congratulate Penny Spencer. However, the playwright looked nonplussed.

TWO

A REVIVED AUDIENCE ROSE from their seats and headed for the back of the hall where trestle tables draped in white linen had been set up, one on each side of the double doors, and stacked with bottles of wine and light snacks. Rex and Helen joined the queue.

"That was a very realistic scream," she remarked.

Several people waiting in line agreed. Rex, for his part, thought it might not prove to be such a dull play after all, but at this point he just felt glad to be able to walk around and stretch his limbs.

"It made my blood run cold, right enough!" said a dapper old gentleman standing in front of them.

"Quite the best part so far," added his female companion, likewise dressed up for the occasion.

"Why did the detectives let the girl go up to the attic alone?" a man behind Rex asked. "And is it a fancy dress? I mean, Sherlock Holmes was a Victorian, wasn't he? And Poirot and Marple were later."

"It's only a play," rejoined a female voice. "You don't have be so literal, Dave!"

"It could involve time travel, I suppose," Dave said, sounding dubious.

Rex turned to find a young couple.

"Anyway, I think it's brilliant," the girl said, smiling back at him.

"Sherlock is as stiff as plasterboard," the elderly man in front commented. "And that Poirot looks all shifty-like, if you ask me."

His female companion chuckled. "I bet you the bumbling Father Brown had the dagger hidden in his cassock all along!"

"I think it's the suitor what got shot, by mistake. He went out to take that phone call just before it happened, remember. Won't the young lady be heartbroken when she realizes what she done!"

"That girl playing Lady Naomi is such a darling. I'm sure she'll go far with her looks and talent."

The line moved forward.

"I'll take white," the old gent told the bartender after confirming the price. "Violet?"

When their turn came, Helen asked for white wine and Rex a red, and they helped themselves to sausage rolls and cheese-and-pickle sticks. As they wandered back towards their seats, balancing their plastic cups and paper plates, Penny Spencer passed in the aisle, an air of preoccupation casting a shadow over her patrician features.

"Well done!" Helen congratulated her. "Quite a cliffhanger!"

"Oh!" Penny said, distracted. "Thank you. Not sure what that loud bang was," she fretted, amethyst earrings jiggling beneath her dark, upswept hair. Rex recalled she had been flushed and nervous when they first entered the hall, where she had stood at the entrance welcoming the spectators. She looked even more flustered now. "It must have been something falling onstage," she concluded.

"It sounded like a shot," Rex said. "Or perhaps a firework."

"Well, it's not in the play. I should probably go back there and find out. You will stay for the party afterwards, won't you, to meet the producer and cast?" Penny asked them both.

"We'd love to," Helen readily agreed.

Rex felt less enthusiastic about having to make small talk with a bunch of earnest theatrical types. However, he wasn't going to throw a damper on things. Penny seemed all right, and Helen was into supporting the arts, especially when someone she knew was involved.

As they reached the front row, a tall, mature man in a greyish-green gabardine suit pushed through the far edge of the velvet curtain and made his way to the lip of the stage, where he asked everyone to please return to their seats until the police arrived.

A murmur lifted in the hall, receding to a lull as the audience waited for details. There had been an accident, the man stammered, his handsome face pasty-white above his black bow-tie, and he begged for everyone's patience.

After he retreated behind the curtain, the hall buzzed and news of the accident spread to the spectators who had temporarily left the hall during the interval. Rex and Helen overheard that the man who had made the announcement was the play's director, one Tony Giovanni. Conversation grew rife with conjecture as everyone wondered what could have happened. Had a piece of stage equipment fallen on someone? Had an actor tripped over and actually broken a leg, as so often exhorted by well-wishers to ward off bad luck? But then, why would the police be involved? Perhaps the gun in Lady Naomi's hand had gone off accidentally. And yet, Rex knew from Penny that no gun was supposed to have been discharged in the play, not even a blank. Most likely it was only a prop, a toy gun.

"Can't someone just go backstage and find out what's going on?" a man in the crowd demanded.

Rex placed his cup and plate on his chair and raised his hands. "Let's all calmly take our seats, as the director requested. I'm sure we'll know what happened soon enough."

"Well, in case we don't," someone stated, "I'm going to grab some nosh before it all disappears."

The last of the audience presently regained their seats and, food and drink in hand, continued to exchange opinions about what might have gone wrong. Some of the spectators claimed to have heard a muffled cry and several people running about onstage within minutes of the scream and the bang, but they had put it down to directions being called out and props being moved for the following act. Rex, who had been with Helen getting refreshments at the time, had not heard anything beyond the scraping back of chairs as people got up amid general conversation.

Yet another person suggested the announcement was all part of the play, a device to add to the suspense, and the notion gained traction for a while. Someone even quipped that the play should have been called *Stage Fright*.

After more than fifteen minutes had gone by, the average duration of an interval, the notion of intentionally misleading the audience for dramatic effect was discarded, and the crowd grew impatient and tense, alternately glancing back at the large double doors in the hall and at the red velvet curtains, which remained resolutely shut, concealing who knew what.

"Should we leave?" Helen asked Rex as they sat sipping the last of their wine. "I could ring Penny later for news. She looks a bit tied-up at the moment."

"I think we should stay. It might be more dire than we think."

Helen swept pastry crumbs off her lap. "I hope you're not suggesting there's been a murder." She almost laughed. "You really do have a one-track mind."

"One of the many reasons you married me, I'm sure."

"More fool me!" she joked.

Mobile phones, which signs posted around the hall had requested be turned off during the performance, were reactivated. Many of the spectators knew someone in the cast, all of whom remained backstage, and frenzied calls flew back and forth. Information was disseminated, compared, and corroborated. Members of the audience moved chairs out of alignment to better converse with neighbours.

Three facts soon emerged: that a death, and not merely an accident, had occurred, followed minutes later by confirmation that the victim was Lady Naomi, played by twenty-four-year old Cassie Chase, and that she had been shot.

Alarm replaced the jittery excitement. Had the gun gone off by mistake or on purpose? A woman in a wheelchair positioned in the aisle fainted. While someone attended to her and another asked around for a doctor or nurse, a man hurried to one of the nearly depleted refreshment tables to fetch the invalid a small bottle of water. It soon transpired through hearsay that she was Cassie Chase's mother, who suffered from multiple sclerosis.

Rex consulted the programme he had discarded on the floor and searched for the bio of her daughter. Cassie had studied drama at the University of Derby and performed in local theatres and festivals, and currently managed an organic bakery. Rex pondered the word "currently" with a heavy heart.

Helen leaned in to see what he was reading. "'Her passions include amateur dramatics, tap-dancing, and her dog Peek-a-Boo, a five-year-old Pekinese,'" she quoted. "It's always the good ones, isn't it? Oh, I hope it's not true. I wonder what she could have done to deserve this?"

"It could have been self-inflicted."

"You mean, accidentally? Or are you saying it might have been suicide?"

Rex had no time to reply. A wail of sirens engulfed the car park of the community centre, and within minutes, ambulance personnel had rushed Cassie's mother out of the hall. The stage curtains rippled and billowed from activity behind them. A handful of uniformed police brought the cast and crew into the hall through the double doors and sequestered them at the back. Rex flexed his fingers. There was little he disliked more than enforced inactivity for extended periods and being kept out of the loop.

"I need to find Penny," Helen announced suddenly.

They found the playwright on her phone by the doors, clutching a cup of white wine, a mottled rash spreading up her neck above the white square collar of her black cocktail dress. She ended her call. "I wish there was something stronger," she said, holding up her drink.

"I'm so very sorry," Helen soothed. "Is it really true about Cassie?"

Penny Spencer nodded with a shuddering sigh. "I was talking to Ron, our producer, just now. He's backstage with the detectives. He was doubling up as prompter, but left before the attic scene because there are no lines in it. He was in the car park and didn't see or hear what had happened until afterwards. You were right about it being a gunshot, Rex. Lady Naomi is actually stabbed in the play."

"Was she shot with the gun she was holding?" Rex asked.

"It appears so. Ron said it was lying by her side. I was very fond of Cassie," Penny went on, barely holding her tears in check. "She was the leading lady and very concerned about getting everything right, and she would consult with me frequently."

Helen put an arm around her. "Such a dreadful thing to have happened. For Cassie's family and friends, naturally, but for you too. I was really caught up in the play."

"It'll have to close now, of course."

Helen gave Penny's shoulders a squeeze. "Is there anything we can do?"

"I told Ron about Rex and his success in investigating murder cases—because what else could it be? The gun we used wasn't real, and I can't believe Cassie committed suicide." Penny shook her head, a puzzled and frightened look on her face. "It just doesn't make sense. Anyway, Ron said he would talk to the lead detective. I hope you don't mind." She looked up at Rex in entreaty.

"Of course he doesn't," Helen replied for him. "Do you, darling? He'll be in his element."

Rex smiled in acknowledgment of this statement. Murders were a nasty business, and would that they never happened. However, the deplorable fact remained that they did, and he felt his knack for solving them should not go to waste. But on the off-chance Cassie Chase had taken her own life, what had driven her to such a desperate act? That, too, posed a mystery. And why would she have done so in front of two hundred people, with an invalid mother in the audience?

He felt his deductive juices going into overdrive. As Cassie's character had declaimed, "Let us get to the bottom of this wretched business without further ado!" And he had every intention of doing so, Derbyshire Police permitting.

THREE

A PAIR OF MEN in plain clothes entered the hall through the double doors at the back and proceeded down the aisle beside the untidy rows of chairs. Standing at the top of the left set of steps leading to the stage, the elder of the two identified himself as Detective Inspector Mike Fiske from Derby North police. His partner was Detective Sergeant Antonescu.

Without further preamble, DI Fiske informed his silent audience that Cassie Chase had been shot, but by her own hand or someone else's had yet to be determined. He asked everybody to remain in their seats for just a while longer. Police officers would be making the rounds to take eyewitness accounts, starting with the front row. Everyone's cooperation would be greatly appreciated, he added. As he was a man of commanding build, it seemed to Rex he was not one to be trifled with lightly.

"Are you Mr. Graves QC?" he asked, approaching. His grey suit was crumpled, his tie askew, and it looked as though he had already had a long day.

"I am."

"Ron Wade, the play's producer, put me on to you. He said you might be a good person to talk to in view of your professional and private experience in such cases. And you must have seen anything there was to see from here." The detective grabbed a spare chair and sat down opposite Rex, his big hands clasped loosely in his lap. "Did you happen to notice anything unusual?"

"Nothing I construed as being unusual at the time," Rex replied. "I must admit to having nodded off briefly before the final scene. We drove down from Edinburgh early this morning," he explained by way of excuse. "I saw the young actress standing onstage holding a gun and the silhouette of a dagger in the background. The curtains closed and a scream rang out. A second later, I heard what I took to be a shot, and assumed as did the rest of the audience that it was part of the play until Penny Spencer, who wrote it, told us it wasn't."

"Can you describe the shot for me?"

"Certainly. It was a dry report, perhaps with a faint echo from the acoustics onstage, loud enough to make me jump out of my skin, but not as ear-splitting as the scream. But that *was* supposed to be in the play, I understand. Although I'm led to wonder, in light of what happened, whether the scream was not all too real…"

"Thank you, Mr. Graves." The inspector produced a spiral notebook from his sagging jacket pocket and scribbled in it with a blue Biro.

"Was Lady Naomi's gun the one that went off?" Rex enquired.

Fiske hesitated before replying. "An old Webley service revolver was found on the floor by her right hand, recently fired. Could that have been the gun you saw?"

"Possibly, but I didn't get a good look. Has Miss Chase's body been moved yet?"

"Very soon, I imagine. The medical examiner is with her now."

"Would it be possible for me to take a quick look?" Rex hoped he did not sound too eager. The inspector shook his head, about to speak, but before he could apologise, Rex interjected. "Seeing the scene of the crime, as it came to be, may help jog my memory."

Inspector Fiske looked at him for a minute as he reconsidered, and then relented with a resigned intake of breath. "Very well, Mr. Graves. Come with me. But I'll have to ask you to keep to the outer perimeter."

Helen, who was being questioned on her side, arched an eyebrow at Rex in knowing amusement as he got up from his chair. "I've known Penny Spencer for about a year," she was telling a uniformed officer.

"So, the playwright is known to your lady friend?" Fiske asked as he escorted Rex to the near set of steps leading to the stage, where a constable stood on guard.

"My wife," Rex corrected, holding up his ring finger. "We were married last weekend."

"Congratulations. First time?"

"For Helen, aye. Getting back to your question, Ms. Spencer teaches French at Oakleaf Comprehensive where my wife was working until recently as a student counsellor. I'd not met Penny until this evening. She is more of an acquaintance of my wife's than a friend. At any rate, Helen did not invite her to the wedding, but possibly because, in the end, we decided to cull the guest list to fifty."

Even then it had been a logistical nightmare, most of the guests having to be put up in hotels near his retreat in the Scottish Highlands, where the reception had been held. Nearly half of them had travelled up from England; his son had flown in from Florida and Helen's father from Australia.

"A lot of fuss and bother, weddings are," Fiske pronounced as the constable stepped back to let them pass. "I've been through three of my own."

He swept aside the curtain, and the two men entered the main stage. The area in front of the grey screen was now brightly illuminated by arc lamps, and paper-suited figures were packing up their equipment.

"Should we be putting on shoe covers?" the inspector called out, and was told that the prints had already been taken.

The scene before Rex looked unreal, more unreal even than the enacted one had been. The dead girl in 1930s dress lay crumpled on the wood floor facing into the set, her right arm flung behind her. A numbered evidence marker stood by her hand, which was protected by a transparent bag.

"The gun's been taken to the lab," the inspector said, following Rex's gaze. "No cartridges left in the cylinder. No exit wound, from what I could see."

Careful to maintain a wide berth, Rex moved around to the far side of the body and peered over at the young woman's face. Golden-brown eyes stared out from beneath false eyelashes, her lips and cheeks enhanced with stage makeup. She looked like a doll, a pretty doll with smooth waves of red hair spread around her head.

Blood had soaked the left side of her white satin blouse and left a sticky patch on the floor. Rex gave an involuntary shudder.

"Shot through the heart," pronounced a man in a white half-mask holding a thick carrying case in his hand. "There's sooting and stippling around the entry wound in a perfect starburst pattern, showing the gun was fired at close range."

"And level," Rex added.

The man turned to him, unhooking the mask from his right ear. "Excuse me?"

"What you said indicates the gun was not angled when it was shot—if it's a perfect starburst pattern."

"Correct."

"Any other injuries, Doc?" the inspector asked.

"Yes, I was coming to that. There's a contusion at the back of the head, presumably from when she fell."

This too suggested to Rex she had been standing. Had it been suicide, he reasoned, the young woman would more likely have been kneeling or sitting on the floor, with the gun in both hands to steady it, especially if she was not used to firearms. Then there was the awkward manoeuvre involved in pointing a gun inwards to one's heart, even if one was right-handed. More probable, she had been shot by someone standing before her, no more than an arm's length away. However, Rex kept these observations to himself as he did not want to be seen as overstepping the mark.

"Right, well, I'll be off," the medical examiner announced. "I should have more for you by Monday," he told the inspector. "I'll let you know then when we can release the body."

"Thank you." Fiske turned to Rex as the man left the stage by the back. "The first thing we checked for was any visible blood on anyone who'd been back here, and we're testing for gun residue on hands and sleeves, including the victim's."

"The butler was wearing white gloves," Rex recalled aloud. "And the lady's companion, Robin Busket, had on leather riding gloves, and Miss Marple a pair of fingerless lace mittens, which I noticed as she knitted away onstage."

"Observant of you. I didn't see the play, of course. None of the actors are wearing gloves now."

"I was trying to determine the time period by the costumes. It was a bit of a hodgepodge."

"Of course, nothing at this point precludes the possibility that Miss Chase turned the gun on herself." Fiske's craggy features softened. "Either way, it's a terrible blow for her mother. It seems Cassie lived at home and helped take care of her."

A good reason for the lass not to have taken her own life, Rex rather thought, adding it to his list of reservations. However, he knew nothing about the victim beyond her brief bio and what he had seen of her playing Lady Naomi—portrayed as a wilful young woman fiercely loyal in love. How this comported with Cassie's real nature, he had yet to ascertain; all being well.

"Shall we?" The inspector led Rex back off the stage and down the polished wood steps.

The noise in the hall had increased in volume as people responded to questions from the police and talked in groups among themselves. Those who had brought flowers to present at the finale now lay them at the edge of the stage.

A pert blonde in a short grey skirt and a multi-hued striped top confronted Fiske, holding a smartphone up to his face. "I'm Cindy Freeman from the *Derby Gazette*."

The inspector declined an interview. He gave Rex his card and strode up the aisle towards his sergeant.

The reporter turned on the Scotsman. "Any comments from you, sir?"

"Did you know the victim, by any chance?" Rex asked. "You're about her age."

The young woman's eyes widened. "Not well," she faltered, clearly taken aback by the question. "I mean, we were at school together, but Cassie was a year ahead. She always had a major role in the school play. I really can't believe she's dead!" Ms. Freeman tucked a short lock of hair behind her ear. "I only came to review the play for my paper. The features editor is now insisting I get a story. This could be a big break for me, but it doesn't seem right, somehow," she added, mostly, it seemed, for appearance's sake.

"Och, you're just doing your job."

"Are you a colleague of Inspector Fiske's? I saw you go up to the stage with him."

"I'm a barrister, an advocate as we call them in Scotland, but I have an interest in solving murders as well as prosecuting those who commit them. I don't know much more than anyone else at this point, and even if I did, I would not talk to the media about it," Rex added with a kindly smile.

"But you saw the body?" the young woman persisted with a catch in her voice, lifting the phone closer to his face.

"Aye, I did. She looks lovely even in death."

"Can I at least quote you on that?"

"If you must, but I didn't see anything amiss during the play."

"I found out from the writer of *Peril at Pinegrove Hall* that the scream was part of the play, but that the shot wasn't."

"She told us the same thing."

"Could I get your full name?"

Rex complied and wished her the best with the story and with her journalistic career, hoping she would not overstate his importance in the case. He found Helen waiting for him by their chairs in the front row.

"Was it gruesome up there?" she asked with a sympathetic frown.

"Not so much gruesome as unreal. In fact, it almost looked staged. Or perhaps it was just an effect of the costume and setting."

"It's tragic, isn't it, especially when you consider that her mother was in the audience? I'm sure Cassie Chase didn't kill herself. Who would do that to their mother, especially since she's confined to a wheelchair?"

"That's what I thought. What's been going on here?"

"The officer asked if I had seen anyone slip out from behind the curtains after the shot went off, which I didn't, and whom I know from the play, and if I could vouch for the person sitting next to me, you included. I told him that one spectator in our row had got up during the play and returned about five minutes later, but that was halfway through the act. I suppose they're checking to see if anyone didn't return before the interval. The ticket attendant was in the lobby and didn't see anyone come in from outside after the play started."

"Who told you that?"

"He was talking to the woman behind us, the one who was complaining about you obstructing her view," Helen murmured, since the lady in question was still in her seat. "Did you learn anything from Inspector Fiske?"

"Aye, he's been very amenable so far."

"That's good." Helen glanced towards the back of the hall. "His subordinate is questioning the cast and stagehands."

"So I see. I think I'll go and take a wee look. Are you all right here for a few minutes?"

"Of course."

The cast members, along with two men in matching tee-shirts and jeans, were assembled in the far corner by the window. Penny stood among them, holding an animated conversation with "Hercule Poirot," whom Rex could see, as he drew closer, was heavily made-up with black eyeliner, pencilled eyebrows, and reddened lips—reminding him of a vaudeville actor.

The long-limbed young man with light brown hair who had played the seductive Henry Chalmers sat weeping in a chair, his face in his hands, while a teary-eyed Miss Marple draped a consoling arm around his shoulders. She had removed her white wig to reveal fading chestnut hair cut in a no-nonsense style, but her lace-trimmed dress in pale blue moiré silk gave her away.

Sherlock Holmes and Lord Peter Wimsey, who had taken off his false nose, lounged despondently against the back wall. The bespectacled Father Brown, cross-legged on the floor in his cassock, dazedly thumbed his phone. A nondescript man, other than having a noticeable overbite, he could have been in his thirties or forties.

Dorkins the butler awkwardly hugged Aunt Clara, who had switched her calf-length black skirt for a pair of purple corduroys and unpinned her dark mane. Rex could not tell if the grey streaks were natural, but either way, Susan Richardson was younger than her character. Rex noticed she kept looking over at Trey Atkins, and there was a depth of feeling in those green eyes. Was it maternal?

The ungainly woman with short, crimped auburn hair who had played her companion conversed with the solicitor by the open window while smoking a cigarette, one hand tucked under her armpit as though she were cold, despite the mild May evening gradually fading outside over the grounds.

The question of who among them had been front-stage when Cassie Chase was shot featured uppermost in Rex's mind as he reviewed each suspect in turn.

FOUR

REX CAUGHT THE INSPECTOR likewise eying the actors, and the distraught young man in particular. Taking advantage of the fact that Fiske was not currently speaking to anyone, he sauntered up to him, hands resting in the pockets of his brushed cotton jacket.

"How was his acting?" the inspector asked, without withdrawing his gaze from the man who had played Henry Chalmers.

"He hardly had any lines in the first act. He just had to act moony. He's after Lady Naomi's fortune, by all accounts, and is a bit of a dandy, but she is naïvely and hopelessly in love, and won't listen to reason. That's about the gist of it."

"I don't think it required a lot of acting on their part. They were going steady in real life."

"Ah, I did wonder." Rex nodded thoughtfully. "That would explain his state of mind now."

The young man, as though sensing he was the topic of conversation, glanced up from his spread hands which had covered his face. He was possessed of regular, if rather sharp, features and lightly freckled fair skin, the whites of his eyes stained red from tears. The lilac silk cravat hung loose about his slender neck. Rex followed the rest of his costume down to his burnt-orange brogues buffed to a mirror shine.

"Trey Atkins, twenty-seven, works in an architect's office," Fiske filled Rex in from his notebook. "I'll give him a couple of minutes to collect himself."

"I have a son close in age," Rex said pensively, hoping for sentimental reasons that the young actor was not responsible in any way for Cassie Chase's death. However, he knew that Trey's close relationship with the victim would make him a prime suspect in a murder investigation. The depth of emotion the lad was displaying was revealing, as well as affecting. That there was a love parallel between the play and real life made the case doubly intriguing.

Rex spotted Helen talking to Penny in a back row of seats, her chair turned sideways in the aisle. Leaving the inspector to get on with his work, he went to join the two women. Those spectators who had been questioned by police were trickling through the double doors, and the crowd in the hall was thinning out slowly. The sound of voices had dwindled to a steady hum, emanating mainly from the far corner of the hall, where the main witnesses were still being interviewed at length.

"Cassie was an only child and her dad passed on when she was eight," Penny was telling his wife, who was good at lending a sympathetic ear.

Rex sat down beside Penny and waited for a pause in the conversation. "Inspector Fiske told me Cassie and Trey Atkins were an item," he said, with a slight query in his voice.

Penny gazed down at the twisted wad of damp tissues in her hands. "I guessed as much, but they played it down, at least during rehearsals."

"Nice lad?"

"The best. The sort you'd want your daughter to be going out with. Trey got on with everybody involved in the play."

"Did everyone else get on?"

"Oh, yes. There wasn't any friction, if that's what you mean; at least not between the cast. I'm sure a lot of backstabbing goes on in the professional acting world, but not here. I wish you could have seen the rest of the play," Penny told Helen. "We video recorded the dress rehearsal, if you'd like to watch it."

"I'd love to."

"So would I," Rex said, significantly more interested in the play in the wake of the tragedy, much as he wished the outcome could have been different. The recording might help give him a better feel for the case. "You said there was no friction between the cast, yet you implied there was some elsewhere…"

Penny gave a light shrug of her shoulders, clad in the black cocktail dress, which Rex could not help but reflect could be one of mourning. "It was nothing, really," she answered. "Just a bit of tension between Ron and Tony Giovanni, the director."

"The tall man in the bow-tie who announced the accident," Rex stated for the sake of confirmation. "I haven't seen him around since."

"He looks rather like an actor, I thought," Helen put in. "And such an operatic name!"

"A lovely man," Penny agreed. "But too shy to perform onstage."

Rex recalled that Tony Giovanni had appeared very flustered, but he had put it down at the time to shock rather than nerves.

"He teaches art at the local primary school," Penny told them, and then confided, "He invited me to dinner once, but nothing came of it."

"Why?" Helen asked, always curious about personal relationships. "You have teaching and drama in common."

"I'm not sure, exactly. He's charming and well-mannered, and all that, but very much a bachelor. I can't really understand why, with his looks. In any case, he didn't ask me out again. I think, if truth be told, he was rather sweet on Cassie, understandably enough. She was a beautiful young woman, without any of those airs that sometimes come with beauty. But it would have been a May-September romance, as Tony is almost fifty, and as Rex mentioned, it seems Cassie was involved with Trey, which was a far more suitable relationship."

"Getting back to his working relationship with the producer ... " Rex intervened before the women could become too sidetracked. "What happened there?"

"Oh, nothing much. Tony, as director and prop-master, was responsible for the creative side of things. Ron took care of the business end, but there was some overlap. For instance, Tony designed the posters and programmes, but Ron had them printed. In fact, Andrew—Andrew Forsythe, who plays Lord Peter Wimsey—he helped with that as he works in a publishing firm. Ron and Tony have been a huge asset, and I was able to give each a small stipend from the grant I received from the arts council."

"Penny won a prize for *Peril at Pinegrove Hall* and was awarded funds to mount the production," Helen explained proudly to Rex on the playwright's behalf.

"It wasn't much," Penny hastened to add. "Just enough to cover expenses, like the printing, and costume rental, and such. I was the official costumier. Much of the furniture you saw was donated or borrowed. Ron is a master scrounger, bless him. But he also wanted to have his say in the aesthetic elements, such as the scenery, which Tony helped paint, and he'd make suggestions on the way the lines were delivered. I have to say I found it a bit irksome myself. After all, I wrote the sodding play. So, I can imagine how Tony felt when he criticized his artwork, like the window in the parlour scene, which I thought was very realistic but Ron said was architecturally inaccurate. But, really, the audience isn't going to know if Pinegrove Hall is Regency or Georgian. The window is in keeping with the mantelpiece, which is all that matters."

"So, you're saying there was a bit of bad blood between them," Rex prompted.

"I suppose," Penny admitted. "But they were mostly civil about their differences, although I think if they weren't being remunerated for their time, one or other of them would have stormed off. Of the two of them, Ron has the more forceful personality, and Tony preferred to avoid a direct confrontation. I'm sure that's why he invited me out that time, so he could vent about Ron. And, I think, to sound me out about Cassie."

"Did you ever have to referee between the two men?" Rex asked, feeling there might be more animosity than Penny let on.

"It never actually came to that. Tony would just roll his eyes behind Ron's back, and sigh, and hum and do all those passive aggressive things. But he never trod on Ron's turf, even if Ron trod on his."

Rex had yet to clap eyes on Ron Wade. He found it surprising, in view of what Penny had divulged, that the producer had not been the one to go onstage and deliver the news of the "accident."

"Ron does what for a living?" he asked.

"He's a sales executive for a pharmaceutical company."

"And the others?" Rex pulled the programme from the pocket of his jacket, fully noticing for the first time the artistic motif on the burgundy cover depicting, in black outline, two halves of an antique goblet shattered by a plunging dagger. He turned to the cast of characters and clicked the top of his ballpoint pen in readiness. Helen took her phone from her handbag and shifted away on her chair.

"Ada, who plays Miss Marple, is a librarian," Penny informed him. "Dennis Caldwell, a.k.a. Hercule Poirot, works in insurance. Andrew Forsythe—Lord Wimsey—is in publishing, like I said. Rodney Snyder, our Sherlock Holmes, owns a flower shop, which he advertises in his bio. Something about a rose."

"'A Rose by Any Other Name,'" Rex supplied, leafing forward to the brief bios, which mainly listed the actors' dramatic training and prior productions. "And Timothy Holden who plays Father Brown? The bio doesn't give his job. It's a bit spare, only two lines."

"I don't think he has much of a *curriculum vitae*. He came to us last-minute as a replacement for Darrell, who quit the play to pursue his acting career in LA. Not really sure what Timothy does, but he rode to rehearsals on a push bike. That could be because he's trying to get fit, I suppose, but I don't think he makes much money. That's all the detectives. The man who plays the butler is Christopher Ells, a medical technician at Royal Derby Hospital. Paul Reddit, the solicitor, is a solicitor in real life, and Trey is a trainee architect. Clara Grove," Penny continued, twisting around in her chair, "the woman in purple trousers over there talking to the inspector, is Susan Richardson. She's a stay-at-home mum with three teenage kids. Who am I missing?"

Rex reviewed the list of characters. "Her companion in the play, Robin Busket."

"Oh, yes. That's Bobbi, short for Roberta. She's Paul Reddit's niece and works for his law firm in some administrative capacity. They're all very nice people. It's certainly not one of them."

"And those two men in casual clothes, being interviewed by the detective sergeant? Stagehands?"

"Bill and Ben, the Flowerpot Men, as we dubbed them. Remember *Watch with Mother*?" Penny made a wry face. "Showing my age there. They do props, lighting, and sound effects. Bill works at a sign shop and Ben is a sound engineer for a local radio station."

Rex finished his round of scribbling. "Does the play become a murder mystery?" he enquired. "I mean, it starts off as a mystery surrounding a stolen heirloom."

"Yes. *Peril at Pinegrove Hall* evolves into a murder case and the five detectives are on hand to solve it."

"Who is the culprit?"

"Don't tell me!" interrupted Helen, who had been busy texting without apparently missing much of the conversation. "I want to watch the recording and try to guess for myself." She slipped her phone back in her handbag. "I was texting Julie to let her know what's going on. She planned on seeing the play tomorrow."

Julie, Helen's best friend since university, taught geography at her old school. Helen had arranged to let out her house to her, and Rex and his wife had spent the afternoon packing boxes in preparation for her permanent move to Edinburgh.

"Well, I'd like to know who the killer is," he countered. "In case it's a question of life imitating art."

"Penny can tell you, but *please* don't tell me."

Rex looked expectantly at Penny. Turning away from Helen, she whispered a name in his ear.

"Interesting." He winked at Helen. "I would never have guessed."

DI Fiske came over to where they were sitting. "Ms. Spencer, you can leave, if you wish. We'll ring you if we need further information."

"I'll take Penny home," Helen proposed to Rex. "If you're staying awhile."

"Aye." He turned to the inspector. "If you have no objection, I'll wait around until my wife returns."

"What about my car?" Penny asked.

"We can collect it tomorrow," Helen assured her. "You shouldn't be driving after the shock you've had."

The women left with the last of the spectators, Rex being the exception.

"Staying to play armchair detective?" Fiske asked blandly.

"Armchair detection has proved quite effective in the past," Rex said, holding up the programme. "Witness Miss Marple and Poirot."

"That's just fiction." Fiske smiled briefly, or it could have been a smirk; it was hard to tell with his crooked mouth. "You have an impressive success rate in your private cases, I hear."

Rex shrugged in genuine modesty. "I just hope this is not the case that proves to be my Waterloo." He gave a heartfelt sigh. "It's always worse when death involves a young person so full of promise and who will be missed by so many."

Fiske nodded solemnly and mumbled, "Indeed. This one's got a lot of attention, and I don't see it letting up. It'll be round-the-clock grind for all concerned."

FIVE

"YOU'VE WORKED A CASE in Derbyshire before, in Aston-on-Trent," the inspector stated, pursuing their conversation and looking Rex squarely in the eyes as though taking measure of him and his abilities.

"That's right. A really messy affair at a wedding reception. It's one of the reasons our own wedding got postponed. But in the end ours turned out just grand." Except for a few minor hiccups. Rex paused. "Ehm, I know it's a bit soon, but do you have any leads?"

"We're in the process of getting alibis from members of the production—who was where when the shooting occurred—and cross-referencing them to see if they check out."

Rex nodded and waited for elaboration, having perceived the inspector to be a courteous if blunt man who would not wish to offend.

With the ghost of a smile, Fiske consulted his notebook. "There were no dress changes for the second act, and so the actors were at leisure to catch a quick break. Miss Marple, Aunt Clara, and Father Brown went to use the conveniences down the corridor before the rush in the interval. The stagehands, them two over there with my sarge, were having a smoke outside the building. Ditto Bobbi Shaw and Paul Reddit—"

"Lady's companion and solicitor in the play," Rex interjected, mostly for his own benefit. He hurriedly added notes to his programme in the absence of anything else to write on. "It's almost like having two sets of suspects."

"Could get a bit complicated," Fiske agreed. "Christopher Ells—Dorkins, the butler—was sneaking a tipple backstage, according to Sherlock. Also backstage was Andrew Forsythe, who plays the ponce detective. Never thought much of Wimsey myself, but my third wife liked Dorothy L. Sayers, in fact all those Golden Age writers of detective fiction."

Rex marvelled in passing at the inspector's literary knowledge, while hoping he would be able to read his scribbles if he needed to later.

"Forsythe was on his phone during the crucial time," the inspector continued, "as was Poirot, as the records show. They can't have been front of stage at seven forty-five, when the shot was fired, according to witnesses. Then we get to Trey Atkins, who says he was waiting backstage for Cassie. He's the one that found her body and called the police, at seven forty-eight. Christopher Ells confirmed she was dead. He works at the big hospital."

"Whose arm was holding the dagger?" Rex asked.

"The image was on a projector. Bill Welsh set it up before leaving for his smoke. His mate Ben Higgins says they left the building together. They think they heard a bang, but couldn't tell where it came from."

"That's a bit strange coming from a sound engineer."

"Perhaps, but getting people to account for their movements after the fact often involves a certain amount of confusion. Sometimes they imagine things. They could already have been outside and not heard the shot at all. Still, we'll be looking into all these people's backgrounds for priors. So far, they appear to have regular jobs and stable family lives, those who are married. And we can't exclude the possibility that Cassie Chase was unhinged. Maybe the strain of caring for her mother along with full-time employment and all the effort she put into the play proved too much for her."

"That still leaves the director and producer," Rex said, consulting his notes. "Penny told me Ron Wade was the prompter, but there were no lines in the last scene before the interval. It was just Lady Naomi alone in the attic." And maybe one other person, he reflected grimly, tapping the pen against his bottom lip. "Where was Mr. Wade at the fateful moment, I wonder?"

Fiske licked his forefinger and flipped back through the pages of his notebook. "Let's see here. I spoke to him first. Says he stood behind the Chinese screen, then as soon as the partition came down for the attic scene, he exited the building to fetch his migraine pills from his car."

"Ah, yes. Penny did mention something about him going to the car park. Did anyone see him there?"

"He thinks so. But he suggested I talk to you, remember. A guilty man would not want the extra scrutiny."

"He did so on Penny's recommendation," Rex pointed out. "I don't suppose he's heard of me."

Fiske's eyes narrowed at the same time as his mouth widened. "But I have, which is why I welcome your input."

"Thank you." Even if the inspector was only tolerating his input, it was more cooperation than Rex had received in some prior cases. Less-seasoned detectives tended to be more territorial than the senior ones, for whom a case solved was a case closed. The top brass didn't care too much how it came about, so long as proper procedures were observed.

"And Tony Giovanni, does he have an alibi?" Rex asked, afraid of pushing his luck but taking the risk since this might be his last opportunity to speak with the inspector in person.

"I've yet to interview him. He's as badly shaken as young Atkins. A paramedic gave him a shot of Valium before I got a chance to talk to him." Fiske surveyed the hall for signs of the director. "I wonder where he got to."

Rex had been wondering the same thing. "Apparently he was rather taken with the leading lady."

"Who told you that?" Fiske asked, turning his head back sharply.

"Penny Spencer. She was a confidante of his." Rex paused as he realized with sadness what tense he had used. "Funny how everything is suddenly referred to in the past," he remarked. "Less than two hours ago everything was moving forward."

The whole play would have been over by now if all had gone according to the general plan. He and Helen would at present be at the reception, meeting the cast. They would no doubt have been complimenting Cassie on her performance, the actress's amber eyes shining, her cheeks flushed from her night of success. Penny would be sharing in the praise as the playwright who had written such an entertaining piece. However, the three-act play had been derailed by someone's more devious plan.

"With a tragedy like this," Detective Inspector Fiske said glumly, "it's always Before and After. My sarge spoke to Ms. Spencer. I'll see what he's got and arrange a follow-up with her tomorrow."

While Fiske went to confer with DS Antonescu, Rex ambled over to Trey Atkins, who sat gazing up at the high ceiling, his head resting against the ecru-painted wall.

"I'm so very sorry for your loss," Rex said, taking the chair vacated by Miss Marple. Ada Card, he reminded himself, glancing at his battered programme. "Do you live close by? My wife left to take Penny home, but she won't be long if you need a lift on our way home." He told Trey where Helen lived and produced his business card from his wallet, purposely dropping it at the young man's feet in order to take a closer look at the carefully laced brogues. He retrieved the card and handed it to the young man, who gazed at it blankly.

His bloodshot eyes then drifted towards Rex. "Thank you, but I'm waiting for Ada. She left her handbag backstage and one of the constables went to fetch it." He spoke wearily, evidently drained and at the point where every minor activity was an effort, even small talk.

"She was perfect in her role, I thought," Rex continued in an attempt to draw him out of his cocoon of misery.

Trey nodded in acknowledgment. "Ada's read all the Agatha Christie books."

"I understand there are quite a few." Fortunate for Ms. Card she worked in a library.

"She's a good sort, is Ada. She's taken me under her wing while my parents are in Hong Kong." Trey brought a paper tissue to his nose and blew into it. Up close, Rex could see he wore tan foundation, which steady tears and the wiping away of them had rubbed from his cheeks, leaving an unnatural pallor and his freckles exposed.

"Are you from the police?" Ada Card demanded, approaching Rex with firm purpose and carrying an old-fashioned black handbag, presumably the one she had gone to recover. She rested a protective, blue-veined hand on Trey's shoulder. "He's not really up to answering any more questions," she said before Rex could reply. "He's coming home with me."

As Trey pulled himself up from his chair, Andrew Forsythe came up to them, top hat in hand. "You taking off?" he asked the pair. Unlike Ada, he had not removed his wig, a tow-coloured affair combed back from his high forehead and temples. Without his beaky nose, his features lacked definition and distinction, having sagged with the onset of middle age.

"There's nothing more we can tell police," Ada responded, while Rex stood back and offhandedly lent an ear.

"Nor I. As I told them, I was on my phone to my wife, which they were able to verify."

"I hope she's feeling better," Ada said in a commiserating tone. "I know she was sorry to miss the play, but in the event, I suppose it's just as well."

"What happens now?" Forsythe asked. "I mean, the play was supposed to run for three consecutive weekends."

Up to this point, Trey had said nothing and simply stared in misery at the floor. Now he looked up and blurted, "It's over, can't you see? It's not as though Cassie can be replaced!" Blindly, he stumbled towards the doors.

Ada hastened after him and grabbed his arm, and Andrew Forsythe followed, head bowed. Suddenly, he turned about and almost bumped into Rex.

"Blast. I forgot my walking stick," he muttered, going back to retrieve it from where it leant against the back wall. He brandished the stick at Rex. "Uncommonly careless of me. My grandfather's, don't you know. Would hate anything happenin' to it."

"It's a very fine cane," Rex took advantage of observing.

"Malacca, and with a silver knob, just like Lord Peter's. Helps me keep in character, what?" Forsythe's long mouth slipped into a grin. He saluted Rex with his top hat. "Good evenin' to you!" he said, and with that, strode off briskly with the unnecessary aid of his cane.

Helen crossed him in the hall as she sought Rex. "He made a rather good Peter Wimsey, I thought," she said, joining him.

"I rather fear he believes he's Lord Peter incarnate," Rex said, gazing after him. "Perhaps just a wee bit eccentric? I wonder if he puts on gentlemanly airs at his publishing house. And how is the writer of the doomed play?" he added, asking after Penny.

"Under a tremendous amount of strain. She feels responsible for what happened, which is quite irrational, of course, but there you are. Are you ready to go home yet?" Helen asked, though far from imploringly, even though she must be tired. Rex, on the other hand, had caught a second wind.

"Aye," he replied with a last look at the few remaining cast and crew.

"Oh, go on," his wife said. "I can see you're still champing at the bit. I had a quick cup of tea at Penny's. I'll be fine for another quarter of an hour."

He kissed her firmly on the lips. "Thank you. You are incontestably one of the most patient women I know."

"Well, I'd have to be," she quipped.

Rex made a beeline for the two men he felt might hold the answer to a pressing question it seemed the good inspector had overlooked. But in Fiske's defence, he had not seen the first act of the play.

SIX

Bill Welsh and Ben Higgins were preparing to leave after their interviews with Detective Sergeant Antonescu who, Rex felt sure, had been keeping his beady eyes on him since he had mounted the steps to the stage with the inspector.

"Fancy a quick pint at t'Bells?" one of the pair, a Yorkshireman by the sounds of it, was asking the other. They might have been brothers, so similar in appearance were they, both with shaved heads and of medium build, sporting maroon tee-shirts with *CREW* stencilled across the back in white letters.

"Too right, but just the one. The missus will be waiting up for the latest news."

"Excuse me, I'd like a word," Rex said, intercepting them before they could reach the double doors leading into the lobby.

"Ey up," the one from Yorkshire warned his friend, just loud enough for Rex to hear.

"I'm not a reporter nor a detective," Rex hastened to explain. "My wife knows Penny Spencer."

"We were just off to the pub if you want to tag along," said the Yorkshireman's friend.

"To drown our sorrows, like."

There was nothing Rex would have enjoyed more than a draught Guinness, but Helen was waiting, patiently, and he rather doubted she would relish going to the pub at this hour.

"Thank you, but this will only take a minute. Are you Bill or Ben?"

The lookalikes chuckled, holding their beer bellies as they rocked back and forth on their trainers.

"Bill, for my sins. Ben's the handsome one," the Yorkshireman joked.

The only significant difference that Rex could see was that Ben wore glasses and Bill's chin sprouted a scraggly goatee. Rex handed each his business card.

"A QC from Edinburgh," Bill read with exaggerated interest. "I could tell right off you were from across the border. What brings thee 'ere then?"

"Penny invited us to the play." Rex decided some extra bona fides were required to gain the stagehands' cooperation. "Detective Inspector Fiske permitted me to see the crime scene."

"Why would he do that?" Ben asked with a puzzled glance at Bill.

"I solve cases in my spare time, what I have of it, and usually only by invitation. Penny asked for my help."

"We just spent the past two hours giving information to t'police," Bill baulked.

"I understand. I was simply wondering how the theatre curtains work." Rex turned towards the expansive panels of red velvet.

Bill's expression visibly relaxed. "Ah, well, as you can see, them's a pair of traverse-style curtains."

"Opening at the centre," Ben explained. "Unlike the guillotine type, which comes straight down."

"They're mounted on a mechanism what operates them at the press of a button."

"A bit like at the dry-cleaner's," Ben added.

These two were a veritable tag team, Rex thought in amusement. "Can you show me?"

"We can't go back there," Ben objected, pushing his glasses back up his bulbous nose. "Crime scene investigators will be all over the stage combing it for clues like they do on the telly."

"They were packing up when I went back there, but I only want to see where the button is located. I'll clear it with the inspector first."

Rex did so, and he and the two stagehands made their way up the steps leading to the stage from the right, accompanied by the constable on guard, who held aside the edge of the curtain so they could enter.

"Please keep to the edge," he instructed. "The centre stage is off limits."

Bill parted the black drapery panels that lined the side wall and showed Rex a red control button situated near the curtains. Rex looked up and saw the track along which they moved back and forth, concealed from the audience behind a valence of red velvet. In the cavernous space above, lighting and sound systems were attached to the crossbeams.

"Is this the only button?" he asked.

"Aye," Bill affirmed.

"Who operated the curtains just before the interval?"

The Yorkshireman scratched a cauliflower ear. "Eh, I was supposed to, but 'appen I forgot."

"You soft pillock," Ben upbraided him mildly.

"Well, someone closed them before the shot occurred," Rex stated.

"Would've been Ron," Ben said. "It's his job to make sure everything's foolproof." He flicked Bill's temple.

The problem with that scenario, Rex considered, was that Inspector Fiske had said the producer left the building before the final scene to fetch his migraine pills from his car. "Why did you forget?" he asked Bill.

"Why does anybody? Ye just do." Bill moved towards a projector set up on a tripod. "I was stood here, and last thing I did was switch this on for t'final scene where t'dagger is projected on yon back scrim. Then I took off for a fag."

"Did you pass anyone on your way backstage?"

"They were all offstage by then, except Cassie, who came up through t'floor. I didn't see nowt unusual."

The trap door was barely visible in the darkness that had redescended on the set after the forensics team had finished processing it. Lady Naomi had stood with her profile to the audience, facing where Rex was now positioned. He stared at the ghostly chalk outline of her fallen body, which had been taken to the mortuary.

He turned to find Bill and Ben gazing on the crime scene in grim silence as the constable stood stoically by, his shoulder radio emitting squawks of static, ready to hold them back if necessary.

"Trey discovered her body and called t'police," Bill murmured, sadly shaking his bald head. "Ee was waiting in t'dressing room and went back to look for her when she never appeared."

"We only found out about the shooting when we got back from our smoke," Ben elaborated. "It was pandemonium backstage, the women crying and everyone asking questions. But nobody knew anything."

"Any sign of Ron Wade at that point?" Rex asked.

"Ee came in soon after we did."

"And the director?"

"Tony was there, white as a sheet and speechless from shock," Ben replied.

"Do you know him well?"

"Bill had more to do with him. They painted all the scenery. I do the sound effects and help shift the heavy stuff around. Tony has a bad back, so he says, and all the lifting was left to us. And Ron likes to micromanage, but doesn't like getting his lily-white hands dirty."

"I've yet to see him."

"You'll know him from his ginger hair," Bill put in. "Bit like your own."

"I was not aware of many sound effects in the play," Rex remarked, reverting to the subject of Ben's duties.

"There were more coming up. The second act starts with dark, melodramatic music as Lady Naomi lies fatally stabbed on the attic floor." Ben's raised fingers prodded the air as he hummed a few bars of a sinister tune. "But she reappears as a ghost."

"Ah. I thought her role might end with the attic scene."

"No, you see her flitting about the parlour in a sheer white dress, invisible to the others while they try to suss out who murdered her."

"So the play contains a paranormal element?"

Ben nodded with enthusiasm. "Right, and it's quite entertaining because only she knows who killed her, but she can't communicate in the normal way, so she resorts to moving objects around and placing clues where the sleuths can't miss them."

"She's a poltergeist," Bill explained. "Might sound a bit daft until you see it. Which like as not you won't now."

"Penny said there was a recording of the dress rehearsal."

"So there is," Bill said. "I forgot."

It seemed to Rex that Bill was rather forgetful.

"Cassie never killed herself," Ben muttered, staring again at the white chalk outline. "She had everything to live for."

"And you were where, precisely, when it happened?" Rex asked in a nonaccusatory tone.

"With Bill outside, or on our way outside. Before that, I was below stage to see that Cassie got up the ladder safely in her narrow skirt and heels, and then I slammed the trap door shut for dramatic effect, but also to make sure she didn't step back without thinking and fall through the opening." Ben spread his hands out in despair. "But it might've been better if she had. The worst thing to happen would've been a broken ankle."

Rex looked about him. If Cassie's death had not been a suicide, the murderer had to have been hiding behind one of the dark panels screening the wall, unseen by Bill. There was nowhere on the set to conceal oneself, and the killer could not have come up after

Cassie through the trap door because Ben had closed it when she stepped onstage.

It was becoming apparent that the shooter would have had to be someone who knew their way around and who knew the play by heart, if their intent had been to murder Cassie undetected and at the very moment her character's death was supposed to occur.

"Presumably there's access from the lobby corridor into the backstage area," Rex probed.

"There's a door into the dressing room, which leads into a storage area behind the stage," Ben acknowledged, while Bill checked his watch, no doubt impatient to get off to the pub.

"I'd like to see it." Rex glanced at the policeman, who immediately requested permission from the inspector on his radio. He reminded them to stick to the edge of the stage and not to touch anything.

They proceeded in single file after Ben.

"Mind how you go," he cautioned in the dim passageway between the stage sets and outer wall.

To their left, the main part of the stage was obstructed from view by rolling panels that provided the parlour scene wall on which was painted the window through which Father Brown had stared forlornly at imaginary rain.

It felt surreal to Rex to be among the props of a play he had viewed from afar earlier that evening, a trifle bored and uncomfortable in his chair. A glancing touch of something cold on the back of his neck made him catch his breath and spin around, but there was nothing and no one close by, the constable a few paces behind and talking on his radio. He dismissed the strange feeling and followed the stagehands into the bowels of the theatre.

SEVEN

BEHIND THE ANTERIOR PANELS of the parlour set, into which the French doors had been cut, lay a narrow space backing onto a fly system of ropes and pulleys for operating the scrims and drops. To the right, a short flight of rubber-covered stairs descended into a storage area where cardboard boxes, loose cables, and tubs of wall paint claimed much of the cement floor.

A stack of large boards, the front one depicting a cobblestone street of half-timbered homes, lay propped against the back wall, beside which stood a crane with a winch.

"They made a reet mess in 'ere," Bill lamented as he surveyed the jumble of props and equipment.

Wheeled racks sheathed in plastic, dispersed willy-nilly across the floor, held an assortment of costumes, one rack containing faux leather doublets, puffy knee-breeches, lace ruffs, and hose, presumably belonging with the crudely painted Elizabethan street scene.

Against the wall by the scenery boards, a row of sloping wood desks tattooed with initials and doodles indicated that Hill Grange

Community Centre had once been a school. The lids, showing evidence of print dust, were labelled with white stickers, one denoting sewing items for the fitting of costumes, another listing the contents as eyewear, false beards, and moustaches. Above the desks, a set of shelves accommodated a musty array of sequined masks and hats and wigs from miscellaneous time periods, along with swashbuckling boots, dress shoes, and heeled slippers festooned with dyed feathers and studded with glass gems.

"An Aladdin's cave," Rex remarked.

"That it is," Ben concurred. "Must be hundreds of fingerprints in here going back years, especially as the caretaker is a lazy old git who never cleans the place properly."

"Not to worry. The investigation is in safe hands with Inspector Fiske and his team," Rex said with a courteous nod towards the constable waiting a short distance away.

Wedged sideways under the stairs stood a table stained with dark circles; upon it, an unplugged tea kettle, a collection of mismatched mugs, and a half-consumed packet of milk chocolate biscuits.

"This here's the trap room." Ben switched on a light located in the alcove and pointed into the space beneath the stage, barely high enough for a man of average height to stand, let alone Rex, without bumping his head on the rafters. "And that there's the ladder leading up onstage."

"Is there just the one trap door?"

Ben nodded.

"And it was just you and Cassie down there?"

Ben nodded again. "It was dark, as we couldn't have light shining up onto the stage for the attic scene. But it wasn't so dark that I couldn't see if someone else was in there." He switched off the light and crossed to a door. "This is the dressing room."

The space in here was redolent of hair lacquer and fitted with four tables and stools lined up beneath mirrors lit by Hollywood bulbs. Packets of cotton wool, pots of Ponds cream, and makeup brushes littered the yellowed laminate surfaces caked and smeared with a rainbow hue of cosmetics.

A series of black curtains suspended from a rod partitioned off one end of the room into four cubicles. In the last one, a pair of glasses with black frames lay on the built-in wood bench. From a peg dangled a green paisley-pattern scarf and matching umbrella.

"Those belong to Susan," Ben said, reaching up for the items.

"Don't touch anything," the constable restated.

"Right, well, that's the lot. This here's the way out." Ben preceded Rex and Bill through a window-panelled door, which the constable locked behind them.

The corridor floor, sealed in drab green linoleum, ended at a push-bar fire exit next to a stairway and ran in the opposite direction past the lavatories and into the lobby.

"Seen enough, Mr. Graves?" Ben asked as Bill made towards the front entrance.

"Aye, thank you." Rex pulled two Bank of Scotland notes from his wallet. "Here you go. Your drinks are on me."

"Ta very much. And good luck finding out what happened to our Cassie," Ben added before hurrying after his friend.

Rex entered the main hall, pleased with his impromptu tour back stage, but unsure whether Helen would feel quite the same way. Patience had its limits, after all.

To his surprise, he found her talking to Susan Richardson, Aunt Clara in the play. Only she among the actors now remained in the hall which, emptied of the earlier crowd, was beginning to feel chilly. No one had thought to close the window beyond which night had descended.

"Susan's daughter Hadley attends Oakleaf," his wife informed him with a bright smile as he approached.

"Pleased to meet you." Rex extended his hand to the woman in the purple corduroys and severe black blouse, clasped at the collar by a coffee-and-cream cameo. She had a shapely mouth covered in an unattractive mulberry shade of lipstick designed, he assumed, to make her look older for her role.

"I was just telling Helen what a lovely girl Cassie was. I can't believe it. None of us can. Helen says you're working on the case." Mrs. Richardson held him in her direct green gaze. "What do *you* think happened?"

"Too soon to say, but a few people I've spoken to who knew Cassie think it impossible she took her own life."

Susan emphatically shook her long, dark wavy hair streaked with grey. "She wasn't depressed or anything this evening, just slightly nervous and giggly like the rest of us before we went on." She stared wistfully towards the red curtains. "Cassie was in her element onstage. She was a natural." Tears welled in her eyes, already smudged with mascara beneath the lower lashes. "What her mother must be going through!"

"Have you met Mrs. Chase?" Rex asked as Helen took a call on her mobile and stepped away, mouthing an apology.

"A few times," Susan replied, making a valiant effort to compose her features. "She and Cassie's aunt came to most of the rehearsals. They were so proud of her. Belinda, the aunt, lives on the same street as her sister and helps take care of her. Do the police think the gun went off by mistake?" she asked in a low voice, although there were few people about to overhear. "But how? Ron insists it was a sham gun. He's the producer and the one who procured it. Cassie would never have exchanged it for a real one. Did someone else?"

"Can you think of anyone who might have?"

"On purpose? Or as a joke? No! Everyone adored Cassie."

"She must have had several admirers," Rex suggested, conjuring up in his mind the brooding director with his dark good looks. "Some secret, some not so secret?"

"Tony was sweet on her in a shy sort of way," Susan said, confirming what Penny Spencer had told him. "He was very—I don't know—solicitous around her."

"And Ron Wade?"

"Ron's a bit of a cold fish." Susan shrugged her shoulders as much as she could in the restrictive black blouse. "Well, he may have fancied her, but he never let on. Anyway, Cassie and Trey were romantically involved," she added casually.

Rex remembered the way Susan had looked at Trey Atkins earlier. "I didn't know that was common knowledge."

"They tried to keep it secret, but I saw them kissing in the car park one night. He's in pieces, naturally."

"Aye, I talked to him earlier."

"I saw you go up onstage with Bill and Ben. Did you find anything?"

Rex shook his head. "Just your glasses and matching umbrella and scarf."

Susan looked startled for a second. "Oh, in the dressing room, you mean. When the play was cancelled, I just had time to get out of the bottom half of my costume before we were all ushered out, and I forgot my scarf and umbrella. But the glasses aren't mine. They were there when I went back to change. They could be Timothy's."

"Father Brown? He was wearing his when I saw him here in the hall."

Susan Richardson pulled back the black cuff of her sleeve and checked her wristwatch. "Goodness. I should get going."

"Us too," Helen said, rejoining them and slipping her phone in her handbag.

The women hugged briefly and Susan took off in the direction of the exit.

"Had enough for one evening?" Helen asked him.

"I have. It's been quite a night."

"I'll say. An actual death on the opening night of a murder mystery play. You do have a knack for being in the wrong place at the wrong time, Rex."

"I perceive it more as being in the right place at the right time." He took her arm and guided her towards the doors. "The timing of the murder, if such it be, *is* significant, don't you think? As though someone were making a statement."

"An act of bravado, certainly. But not on Cassie's part. There's nothing I've yet heard about her to suggest she was unbalanced or selfish enough to seek momentary fame by committing suicide on-stage."

"And literally staging her own murder to disguise it was suicide?"

Helen looked doubtful. "Do you honestly think that's a possibility?"

"I think it more likely someone was waiting in the wings and staged her suicide. Here might be the right people to ask."

Inspector Fiske and his sergeant stood together in the pool of light beyond the building's entrance, looking up as Rex came through the glass doors. He was conscious of Antonescu's gaze upon him, the black of his deep-set dark eyes enhanced by his almost translucently pale complexion.

"Any joy, Mr. Graves?" Fiske enquired amiably enough.

Rex paused in front of him, hands thrust in his jacket pockets. "It strikes me that Tony Giovanni is the missing link thus far."

"Why's that?" Fiske asked, while his sergeant shuffled his feet on the patio, making his presence and impatience felt.

Helen, buttoning up her raincoat, said she would bring the car around.

"Giovanni is the only person who might legitimately have closed the theatre curtains at the end of the first act in Ron and Bill's absence," Rex answered the inspector.

"The Yorkie stagehand with the goatee?" Antonescu enquired, his own chin immaculately shaven, the sort of man, Rex imagined, to carry an electric razor about his person at all times.

"The same." Rex turned back to Fiske. "He said he forgot to press the button and that Ron, who oversaw the production, must have done so. But if Ron left before the attic scene to go to his car, he would not have had time to go back and see to the curtains. And no one else puts themselves front of stage in the minutes leading up to the shot. So, unless Giovanni or the Phantom of the Opera—of the play, in this instance—pushed the button, it must have been someone who does not want to be identified as the killer or as a key witness."

"The director would be a logical choice for the curtains," Fiske acknowledged. "Or the other stagehand."

"Ben was working below stage."

Fiske scratched the incipient stubble on his jaw. "Giovanni said he was backstage the whole time. I spoke with him by phone. He's at home recovering from the shock of what happened."

"The artistic temperament," Antonescu put in with a sardonic smile.

"He told me he was drinking tea with the stagehands in the storeroom," Fiske went on to inform Rex. "By the time Ben Higgins went to open the trap door and Bill left to lower the screen and work the lights and projector for the attic scene, the actors were all coming offstage. Trey Atkins, as Henry Chalmers, was the first to come down, and he saw Giovanni and the stagehands. All the actors had been onstage during the first act or waiting to go on, I'm told. But the butler was mostly off than on. He could see the director at the table looking as nervous as the actors felt on the opening night."

A promising alibi for Tony Giovanni, Rex conceded, impressed by the inspector's power of recall and his succinct summary. But if the director was in the clear, perhaps he had seen something while sitting by the back stairs and keeping an ear out for possible signs of trouble with the play. During that time, Ron Wade had been in the midst of the action behind the Chinese screen in case someone forgot their lines. All eventualities covered.

And yet, apparently not. Bill Welsh, if he was to be believed, had scarpered before attending to the curtains, and minutes later, Cassie Chase was dead.

If Fiske had been alone, Rex might have ventured to ask for an opportunity to speak with the elusive director, and then Helen's Renault pulled up in front of them, and he took his leave.

"Was the inspector of any help?" his wife asked as they drove past the fleet of blue-yellow-and-white police vehicles and through the redbrick gateposts.

"Up to a point, but he doesn't have the benefit of having seen the play."

"Now you can watch the whole thing," Helen said encouragingly. "Penny gave me the DVD of the dress rehearsal. It's in the glove compartment."

Rex smiled at her in the dimly lit car. "If we watched it tonight, I could offer to get it to the inspector tomorrow. Then perhaps I could gain access to your heartthrob, Tony Giovanni."

"Heartthrob, indeed! I just said he looked like an actor and had a lovely name. You know, if we're going to watch the play, I'll need sustenance. Fancy some Indian take-away? There's a Tandoori place just up the road. See that big orange sign?" Helen made a ruefully apologetic face. "It seems awful to be hungry at a time like this."

"Quite normal, I think. That's why there's always a pile of food at funerals."

Rex thought of the young woman on a mortuary slab and wondered again at the brazen killer who had put her there; for nothing he had learnt so far pointed to an accidental shooting or suicide, even if the players did appear to all have convenient alibis.

EIGHT

"I'm trying to remember what I did with the DVR player," Helen said as they unpacked the foil-lidded cartons of Indian food in the kitchen.

"I put it in one of the boxes," Rex told her. "I'll hook it back up."

"I'll see to this. You know, if you are going to pursue this case, we'll never get the packing done."

"Och, so what? Julie's not going to be using our bedroom, is she? Why not store up there what we're not taking with us back to Edinburgh until we're next down for a weekend?" In Rex's view, Julie's judgment could not be trusted when it came to men, and piling the room with boxes would help keep her out while freeing up some of their time.

"That's called procrastinating," Helen said with a smile.

"I believe it can sometimes be referred to as sensible time management."

With the DVR set up in the entertainment unit, and the coffee table spread with a late supper, Rex loaded the disc and installed himself on the sofa beside his wife.

"Ready?" Taking up the remote, he started the DVD.

The familiar red bi-parting curtains opened on the parlour scene and the group of detectives began speaking in turn. Fortunately, the recording, both video and audio, proved of adequate quality.

He took up his bowl of aromatic curry and rice. "At least Cassie's mother will have this to remember her daughter by."

"One day, when she can bear to watch it."

"Did Penny say when the dress rehearsal was held?"

"The day before yesterday. Wednesday." Helen nodded towards the spinster detective in the blue silk dress and dainty lace-up boots. "My money's on the elderly lady wielding her evil knitting needles," she whispered darkly, in an attempt to lighten the mood.

"Are we talking Jane Marple or Ada Card?"

"Well, I suppose either could have concealed the murder weapon in that black bag beside her. The dagger in Miss Marple's case, the gun in Ada's."

The handbag on screen was the same one Ada had taken home with her as she escorted Trey out of the hall. "It's not Miss Marple," Rex divulged to Helen. "I can tell you that much."

"You're not supposed to tell me, remember," Helen remonstrated, chucking a piece of poppadum at him.

"I may just be misleading you."

"You're incorrigible, you know that?"

"Aye, you've told me often enough. You said it was the main reason you agreed to marry me."

"Ri-ight," his wife responded with playful sarcasm. "Anyway, if I were Cassie and didn't intend to kill myself, I wouldn't be holding a loaded gun. But then, I'm petrified of guns," Helen stated, tearing off some naan bread and spooning a dollop of mango chutney on it. "Penny said theirs was a relatively light replica. If it was switched at the last minute, Cassie would surely have noticed."

"Maybe she did notice, but it was thrust into her hand and she had no time to react, needing to get on with the next scene. Though I agree it's more likely she was standing onstage with the prop, and the killer substituted it for the real gun after he shot her, no doubt having wiped off any fingerprints first. Let me just check something."

Rex fast-forwarded to the attic scene and paused the disc on Lady Naomi pointing a revolver in her right hand. He got up from the sofa and crouched in front of the television screen but still couldn't make out any details, even with the aid of his reading glasses. From what he could see, however, the gun in the dress rehearsal looked like the one he had seen in the play earlier that evening. He pressed *play* and the red velvet curtains closed on Lady Naomi maintaining her pose. Behind the joined curtains came a scream. And then silence. He replayed the attic scene without pausing.

"Did you notice that Cassie holds her pose for a shorter duration than she did tonight?" he asked Helen, who nodded in agreement. "In the dress rehearsal someone must have closed the curtains on cue."

And something else: if Cassie had been using the replica gun tonight, where was it now? Rex wondered if Inspector Fiske would mind very much if he rang him to find out if it had been found, but when he consulted Helen on the subject, she categorically advised against it. The inspector might be asleep, she argued, or else eating a late dinner with his wife, just as they were. Rex informed her that Fiske was divorced from his third wife, and Helen retorted that she could see why: the poor man was probably beset by calls at all hours.

Rex capitulated. He didn't want to make a nuisance of himself and ruin the rapport he had built with the inspector. It would have to wait until tomorrow. He rewound the DVD to where they had first left off, with Miss Marple wittering on about the attic as a possible place for the thief to have hidden.

By the end of the first act he had gleaned nothing further with regard to the murder, except the order in which the actors had left the parlour. This he had missed at the theatre when he nodded off after Henry Chalmers was called away by the butler to take a phone call offstage. Aunt Clara had then retired to her room with a headache, accompanied by Robin Busket. The solicitor had followed on their heels, presenting his excuses to the detectives and saying he needed to ring his office. And Lady Naomi, with a dramatic sigh of impatience, had taken herself off to the attic. The scrim had then descended on the five sleuths discussing the case in the parlour.

Helen sat back on the sofa with a satisfied and knowing expression. "Aunt Clara's companion, Robin Busket, is really a man. He's the murderer in the play."

Rex smiled and nodded. "I'm impressed, and we've only seen Act One. Penny told me it was Robin. How did you know?"

"The first clue is the name. *Bosquet* is French for 'grove'. Robin Busket has to be related to Naomi and Clara Grove of Pinegrove

Hall, presumably built when their aristocratic ancestors fled France during the revolution and resettled in England, bringing their most treasured possessions with them. And the solicitor mentioned an indiscretion. The Marquis de Bosquet presumably had an illegitimate son, Naomi's half-brother, who has ingratiated himself with Aunt Clara and become a member of the household so he can find an opportune moment to steal the goblet and murder the heiress."

"A bit of a cheap trick if you don't know French," Rex contested.

"Well, there are other clues. Robin's manly gait, for instance. She said she'd been thrown by a horse, a stallion, no less, and had sprained her ankle, but she looks able-bodied enough to me. And she over-compensates as a woman in her mannerisms. 'Oh, my dear this!' and 'Oh, my dear that!'"

"I thought it was just bad acting."

"There'll be other clues in the rest of the play. Shall we?"

They continued watching, and Rex tried to follow the complexities of the plot to its conclusion whilst focused on the actors and their demeanour. Henry Chalmers, on whom suspicion of the theft had fallen in Act I, was exonerated when Robin Busket was finally unmasked by Miss Marple for the very reasons Helen had enumerated, helped along by Hercule Poirot's little grey cells. Contributing, too, were Wimsey's airily astute observations, Sherlock's keen powers of deduction, and a dose of divine intervention, thanks to Father Brown, in the form of Lady Naomi's ghost. Aunt Clara had felt "chills" when Lady Naomi's avenging spirit was in the room, the spirit ultimately tripping up the aunt's companion by placing a footstool in her path, resulting in jewels from the stolen goblet spilling from the imposter's riding boot and ultimately forcing Robin's confession to the heroine's murder. "Under our roof the whole time!" Aunt Clara had exclaimed in a fit of vapours.

Henry Chalmers, whom Naomi had valiantly sought to protect right up to the end, was not only spared the hangman's noose but inherited her estate through a secret will she'd had drawn up, and which the solicitor revealed in the final scene, whereupon Henry declared he would forever stay true to the memory of his dear, departed betrothed. The vying detectives refused any reward for their services. As Hercule Poirot put it, having the last word, "*Noblesse oblige.*"

"Some of the acting was a bit wooden, but, overall, a pretty flawless production, I thought," Rex said at the end. He lifted his tea mug. "Kudos to you, Mrs. Graves, for solving the mystery before the second act."

"You might have done, too, had you been paying more attention the first time around."

Rex had hoped she had not noticed his lapse at the theatre. "I'll try to redeem myself by solving the real mystery," he told her with a sheepish smile. "And you were right when you said it was never the butler. But could it be in real life? Dorkins never reappears in the first act after he summons Henry Chalmers into the hall for the phone call. Inspector Fiske relayed to me that Christopher Ells saw the director in the storage area, but who saw what Ells was up to?" Other than Rodney Snyder, a.k.a. Sherlock, who had reportedly seen him downing some liquor during the interval, as Rex recalled the inspector telling him.

"I'm sure you'll get to the bottom of it." Helen planted a loving kiss on his lips. "But kudos really to Penny and everyone involved. It's no mean feat to pull off a play like this, especially on a shoestring. It must have been very satisfying to see it all come to fruition." She gazed back at the TV. "It's a shame the actors never got a real curtain call."

The screen was frozen on the eleven players strung across the front of the stage, hands linked, in the process of taking a bow, with Lady Naomi in the middle, Henry Chalmers to her right, and Poirot to her left, emphasizing the disparity in their heights. Cassie was close to five nine in her heels, judging by Trey Atkins, whom Rex had stood beside earlier and estimated to be at least six foot tall, whereas Dennis Caldwell, who played the Belgian detective, did not top five five.

"What are you staring at?" Helen asked.

"I'm wondering why they placed a short man beside a tall girl. In fact, all the women are tall except for Miss Marple. It might have looked better if Poirot and Father Brown had stood on each end."

"Poirot was probably given a prominent place because he's the funniest actor."

"By virtue of being so ham? He's no David Suchet."

Helen yawned into her hand. "Well, either way, he got a lot of laughs this evening."

"Yesterday evening," Rex corrected, glancing at the carriage clock on the mantelpiece. "It's hours past our bedtime." He stretched his arms above his head. "I'll clear the dishes. I've kept you up long enough."

It had been a long day for them both. When they had set out from Edinburgh, he had never entertained the prospect of a real murder.

NINE

THE NEXT MORNING AFTER breakfast, Rex was able, after several tries, to make contact with Inspector Fiske who, albeit sounding weary, was as cordial as before. In answer to Rex's enquiry, he said the replica gun had not yet been retrieved. The one used in Cassie Chase's death had been shown to Tony Wade in its evidence bag the previous evening, and the producer was adamant it was not the one he had bid for on eBay and which had been used in the rehearsals. The prop, although similar, had been made of plastic, according to Wade.

Inspector Fiske told Rex that the police were conducting a search of the Chase residence, not only for the missing prop but for any indication at all of Cassie's frame of mind.

"Such as a suicide note?" Rex asked.

"That would certainly be helpful, but any leads pointing to what happened last night would be welcome." The inspector concluded by reminding Rex to keep all information he had passed on as confidential.

Rex assured him he would and asked if he had seen the DVD of the dress rehearsal. "My wife and I watched it last night," he explained. "I can't say that anything really leapt out at me, but it was useful as context."

"Penny Spencer mentioned such a recording to my sergeant. Did she give you her only copy?"

"I'm not sure, but you're welcome to it."

"If there's any way you can return it to her in the course of the morning," Fiske requested, "I'll be visiting her after lunch."

Rex agreed to do just that, glad of the opportunity to speak to Penny again. He was about to broach the question of Tony Giovanni when Fiske said he had to get off the phone and attend to a witness. Rex reluctantly ended the call, wondering who the witness might be and how much further ahead than himself the inspector was in the case.

Tapping the mobile phone against his beard, he contemplated the fate of the replica gun. The police would presumably comb the roads radiating out from the community centre, in case the killer had thrown it out of a car window. However, Rex doubted the person who had managed to avoid detection thus far would have been so careless as to get rid of evidence close to the scene of the crime. More probably, it had been disposed of in a body of water, or else smashed to smithereens and scattered to the four winds. But how had it been smuggled out of the building? All cast and crew members would have been searched before they left.

"More coffee?" Helen asked, poking her head into the sitting room.

"Thanks, but I've already had two mugs." Rex heaved himself out of the cushy armchair and stretched his arms in front of him. "Inspector Fiske asked me to return the DVD to Penny. Are you coming?"

Helen hesitated. "I should really carry on with the packing. I'm in the process of wrapping up some small items." She had agreed to leave the less important boxes in the bedroom until their next visit rather than try to arrange for a moving van over the Spring Bank Holiday weekend.

"I can drop off the two crates at Oxfam. Anything else I can do while I'm at it?"

"If I give you a list, can you be a love and take care of the shopping? And I'd better give you Penny's address."

Rex decided to go there first and leave the errands for later. Once the car was loaded with the charity donations, he set off for the neighbourhood where Penny lived, close to the community centre in a residential street filled with newer two-storey homes clad in white wood and enclosed by tall hedges. A red estate wagon was parked in the driveway. Rex somehow doubted the lacklustre vehicle belonged to the sophisticated Penny Spencer. If she had a visitor, he would have to just drop off the DVD and leave, more the pity. He rang the doorbell.

Within seconds he heard clicking footsteps approaching from inside and Penny answered the door, dressed in a light, oatmeal-coloured jumper and slacks, the same look of chic about her as before, due in part to the silk scarf in shades of brown and amber flowing from her neck. She appeared more composed than the previous night and had a bit of colour in her cheeks. "Oh, hello, Rex." She glanced around him. "Is Helen not with you?"

"She's busy packing. I came to return the DVD." Rex handed it to her. "We couldn't wait to watch it and enjoyed it immensely."

"I'm glad. Do come in." Penny stepped back from the doorway.

"I don't want to impose if you have company."

"Nonsense. You can meet Tony, the director of the play. You might find it helpful to talk to him, and I just made tea."

What excellent timing, Rex thought, closing the front door behind him. "Did you need a lift to the community centre to get your car?" he asked, following Penny as her mules clacked back through the stone-tiled hall.

"It's in the garage. It was sweet of Helen to offer last night, but Tony drove me over this morning."

Bully for Tony. Rex felt a bit of a let-down. It would have been a convenient excuse to go back to the community centre and see if the police were still milling about looking for clues in broad daylight. However, this minor setback was far outweighed by the opportunity to speak with the play's director.

"We're through here." Penny led him into a stylish and sparely furnished sitting room where Tony Giovanni occupied one end of a low trestle settee, his long legs almost folded to his chin. Gone were the gabardine suit and bow-tie, replaced by a light denim shirt worn over a pair of beige khakis and loafers.

Penny introduced Rex as the husband of an ex-colleague at her school, and the two men shook hands. She urged Rex to sit down and he smiled pleasantly at Tony a few feet away, waiting for him to open the conversation.

Despite the director's fifty years, he projected a certain boyishness, which Rex attributed to the barely greying mop of dark hair and widely set brown eyes. Above these grew a pair of thick eyebrows with a few stray white hairs straggling at the outer edges.

Penny filled the silence by asking Rex if he would like milk and sugar in his tea, and then left to fetch another cup for herself. Rex explained that he had stopped by to return the DVD of the dress rehearsal.

"How was it?" Tony asked, balancing his teacup and saucer on raised knees. "I haven't seen it yet."

"Very professional, but rather poignant under the circumstances. Cassie looked so vibrant, as though she had the whole world at her feet."

Penny went to sit beside Tony on the low sofa.

"She had an aura about her," Tony agreed. "Cassie was one of those people you just enjoy being around."

"Hard to believe that only two days later the lass would be dead, let alone through suicide."

"You just never know," Tony murmured, contemplating his teacup.

At this rather enigmatic statement, Rex glanced at Penny, who gave him a tiny shake of her head as though in warning.

"Mr. Graves is helping the police," she said in the awkward pause that ensued. "He's a private detective when he's not prosecuting criminals at the High Court in Edinburgh."

"I'm not acting in any official capacity," Rex hastened to add. "I just happened to be attending the opening night with my wife."

"Helen kindly drove me home last night." Penny turned to Rex. "We're all going to miss her so much at the school."

Meanwhile, Tony had been nodding mutely at his teacup. Rex despaired that he was going to get anything out of him. The director acted as though he was the only person affected by Cassie's death. In fact, he had been the only one involved in the play not to stay behind the previous evening, having been sedated by a paramedic and taken home.

"Was it you who recorded the dress rehearsal, Tony?" Rex asked politely.

Tony looked up in surprise. "No, I was watching with Penny from the front row. It was probably Bill or Ben."

"Ben gave me the DVD," Penny said. "I haven't had a chance to see it yet. The actual rehearsal went off without a hitch and we all went off to the pub to celebrate." Her face crumpled and she looked as though she might cry. She grabbed a tissue from a box on the coffee table and quickly dabbed under her eyes.

Tony started to reach out to her but changed his mind, returning his hand to his lap. Rex was getting the distinct impression he was in the way, and he deposited his teacup in preparation to leave. First, though, there was something else he needed to ask the director.

"Regarding the stage curtains, do you know who closed them last night at the end of the first act?"

"That would have been Bill."

"And you were where at the time, if I might ask?"

"Backstage, sitting at the table in the cubbyhole under the stairs. I was working on some lesson plans in an effort to distract myself. I was probably as jittery as the actors. When they all came offstage and gave me the thumbs-up, I breathed a sigh of relief. Act One was almost over, and Cassie didn't have any more lines. I really thought it would be plain sailing from there." Tony bit down on his lip, staring morosely at his cup.

"Was Ron Wade among the actors coming offstage?"

"I think so. His job was over for the first act."

"Is it possible you might have missed any unusual comings and goings while you were preparing your lessons?" Rex pursued.

Tony sat back on the settee and stared over Rex's head, his symmetrical face skewed in an expression of concentration. "I was facing the back of the stage keeping an ear cocked for any pauses in the dialogue. Ron was prompting, but he's not always very quick off the mark. Usually one of the actors improvises if someone freezes up. But it all seemed to be going well. No, I didn't hear or see anyone go up the steps, if that's what you're getting at."

"And at the time of the shooting, were you still at the table?"

The director bent double over his cup, as though afflicted by physical pain. Penny grasped his hand, and he answered hoarsely, "Yes, and I heard the shot, of course, but I had no idea what it was. I thought maybe one of the speakers in the fly space had crashed to the floor. At that point, I looked around for Ben, but remembered he had left with Bill for a smoke. Oh! So maybe Bill didn't operate the curtains after all. Anyway, I opened the dressing room door. Trey was there fixing his stage makeup and I asked if he had heard the noise, and he said he had. That's when he went up to the stage and found Cassie."

"Who else was backstage with you when the shot rang out?"

"The male detectives," Tony replied, straightening up again. "Except for Timothy Holden, who plays Father Brown. A couple of them were on their phones making it difficult to concentrate on my work. And Christopher, the butler, was on the steps, knocking back gin from a flask. I wasn't too worried at that point because he didn't have much to do in Acts Two and Three. By the time I spoke to Trey, Christopher and the others had already gone up the stairs to investigate. Trey pushed past them, and I followed. The rest of the cast and crew returned in dribs and drabs after that. That's all I can remember, really. It's almost word for word what I told Inspector Fiske."

Rex nodded in thanks and smiled at Penny. "I should really get going. I have to drop some stuff off at Oxfam. Incidentally, I don't suppose either of you have any use for an old VCR Helen is getting rid of?"

They shook their heads. Penny rose from the settee. "Such a hassle, moving; isn't it? I had a lot of stuff to bring over from Paris."

"At least most of the furniture is staying." Rex got up too, and Tony noticeably relaxed as they exchanged farewell greetings.

"Did you get the information you wanted?" Penny asked in a low voice when she and Rex reached the hall.

"Not sure," he replied truthfully.

She accompanied him out the front door and into the soft morning sunshine. "Tony lost a sister to suicide," she confided. "That's what I was trying to signal to you. It's a touchy subject."

"No wonder he was so upset last night."

"Yes, it must have brought it all back. And I was afraid he would suffer another anxiety attack just now."

"When did it happen? The sister's suicide, I mean."

Penny walked him to Helen's car. "When she was eighteen. It was just before her A Levels. A long time ago, but, still."

"The pressure of exams?"

"Tony didn't say. Only that she took an overdose of sleeping pills and no one found her in time. Tony had to break the news to their parents who were away in Spain. He felt responsible because he was supposed to be looking after her."

Rex gave a low whistle. "I see."

"He told me this morning. I think Cassie reminded him of Gisella, and that's why he took her death so hard." Penny gazed at the gravel at her feet. "I thought he was smitten by Cassie. Now I know it was something else." She looked wistful, almost hopeful, and Rex understood better the feeling he'd had in the sitting room of interrupting something between her and Tony.

"Cassie's death may not have been a suicide," he pointed out. "You said so yourself."

"I think, either way, Tony feels he should have been better able to protect her. I suppose we all feel that way. She was the youngest member of the cast. Not that she wasn't mature for her age. She was. But if she didn't shoot herself, who did? I almost find the idea of murder harder to contemplate. I mean, who would do such a thing? I've been thinking about it all night."

"Were you able to come to any conclusions?"

Penny tilted her head, causing her loose knot of dark hair to slip to one side. She raised her hands to secure it. "It has to have been someone with ready access to the stage, someone who would not have alerted suspicion, don't you think?"

Rex smiled at her. "I'd almost forgotten you'd written a murder mystery play. Aye, I agree, and I'd go so far as to say the perpetrator would have had to have acted with a cool head and perfect timing. Let me know if anyone comes to mind."

"Well, not Tony, for starters. You can see for yourself he could never do anything like that."

Rex could not quite agree with Penny there. Tony might not say boo to a goose, perhaps, but a man with a sensitive nature could murder a woman if he'd had his feelings hurt badly enough. Tony may have treated Cassie with brotherly regard, or he may have wanted something more.

"I should be getting back," Penny said, rousing herself to action. "He'll be wondering where I am." She gently touched Rex's arm. "Thank you for helping."

"Of course. Well, goodbye," he said, opening the driver's-side door of the Renault.

"Drop by again with Helen if you have time before you leave for Edinburgh."

He said he would and lowered himself into the car seat, turning the key in the ignition as Penny began walking back to the house, her silk scarf billowing lightly behind her. A nice woman, he thought, reversing out of the driveway. Perhaps if her budding relationship with Tony bloomed into love, something positive could come out of the tragedy.

His mind then switched to the more practical matters at hand. Oxfam first, and then Sainsbury's, he decided, only wishing he had as good an idea of where he was going next in his investigation. Inspiration struck as he pulled out onto the road. He would buy Helen some flowers. He knew just the place.

TEN

REX FOUND A ROSE by Any Other Name tucked between a news-agent and an off-licence. A decorative wind chime on the door tinkled as he entered the shop, and he was immediately assailed by the heady scent of cut flowers, which abounded everywhere in an explosion of colour, tiered rows of almost every variety arranged in transparent plastic buckets. It appeared he was the only customer.

Rodney Snyder stepped out from behind a tall rack of quality greeting cards, instantly recognizable as the man who had played Sherlock Homes, even though he had swapped his Inverness cape and tweeds for a brown canvas apron that covered the front of his shirt and the top half of his trousers.

"Hello, don't I know you from somewhere?" he asked affably, in marked contrast to the acerbic Holmes of yesterday, and quite un-like Andrew Forsythe, who seemed to have difficulty shaking off his Wimsey character. "Have you come for flowers?"

"Partly."

"What sort of thing are you looking for? Is there a special occasion?"

"More spur-of-the-moment." Rex surveyed the vast selection. "I'd like something romantic and cheerful."

"Tulips? You can mix and match. Perhaps a bunch of carnations, irises, and freesias?"

Rex noted an undercurrent of flat Essex vowels, which Snyder had managed to transform into a cultured accent for Holmes. As was the case with most of his flowers, Rodney Snyder appeared to be a transplant from warmer climes south of Derby.

Rex wandered to the large section of roses in every shade, from white to blood-red. "A dozen of these pink-tinged yellow ones, I think." Like most shop-bought roses, they did not give off much of a fragrance, but they would appeal to Helen, who had once remarked that pink and yellow were "happy" colours.

"Do you prefer open or buds?"

"Buds, so they'll last longer?"

Rodney Snyder's gloved hands duly selected a handful of furled roses, dewy-fresh and flawless, and wrapped them in stiff cellophane tied off with a pink bow. "A card to go with?" he asked.

"I don't think so. I trust my own words will not fail me."

Snyder smiled, baring a set of even teeth. "Indeed. The best sentiments come straight from the heart, don't they?" He tactfully did not ask whom the roses were for, even though Rex's silver wedding band was much in evidence as he drew out his wallet at the counter and sifted through his cash. No doubt, not all the florist's married clients were buying flowers for their spouses.

"However, I wonder if you can help me in another matter."

Snyder regarded Rex with sly interest. "This must have something to do with last night. I saw you with the redoubtable inspector. It was obvious you were more than just a witness."

"Unfortunately, I was not much help in that regard. I had a front row seat, but can't say I saw anything worth reporting. I'd be more interested to know what went on behind the scenes."

"Yes, I heard you do a bit of Sherlocking yourself. Even as that most esteemed detective, I couldn't offer much to Inspector Fiske either. I was checking my messages and emails backstage when the shot went off. Andrew and Dennis, two of the other sleuths, were with me," Synder volunteered. "And Tony."

"Christopher Ells was with you too?"

"Oh, that's right." Snyder mimicked taking a surreptitious gulp of something from an upheld hand. "Christopher rather likes his drink. Hope he doesn't do it on the job," he added in a snide tone.

"Which is what, again?"

"Something at the hospital. An orderly or lab technician or some other low-level position, but still."

"So, it was just the five of you backstage when the shot was fired?"

Snyder nodded. "Plus young Trey. He came in from the dressing room. The others, except for Cassie, of course, had left. The notion of a gunshot never seriously occurred to me. We went to investigate, to make sure she was all right. But, regrettably, it was curtains for Cassie."

Snyder struck Rex as rather glib in his reaction to her death. "Aye, it was."

At that moment, a flustered woman entered the shop and asked about a bridal bouquet for her daughter. Rex lifted his hand to the florist in a gesture of thanks and goodbye.

"Ta-ra." Snyder pointed to the roses in Rex's hand. "Enjoy."

Rex left the shop and drove off down the street to continue his rounds, first to deposit the donations and then to take care of the shopping. He arrived back at Barley Close with three filled bags from the supermarket and hauled his purchases through the front door of Helen's 1930s semi-detached house.

"Guess who I ran into at Oxfam?" he asked as she took one of the bags into the kitchen.

"Who?"

"A younger Aunt Clara. Well, I didn't see Susan Richardson to speak to. She was driving off when I arrived. I thought it a bit curious that she'd be there the morning after Cassie's death, so I asked at the collection desk what she'd brought in."

"You were dropping off stuff, so why not she?" Helen pointed out, taking the vegetables out of the shopping bag she had deposited on the counter. "What did she donate?"

"A box of clothes. Teenager stuff, mainly." Rex set his remaining load on the floor by the refrigerator.

"Well, then. Presumably, her youngest has outgrown the clothes, and she decided to de-clutter."

"Aye, but her purple trousers, the ones she was wearing yesterday, were in the box as well."

Helen paused in her sorting of items. "That is a bit peculiar, like you said. Perhaps she wanted to get rid of them because they reminded her of what happened."

"Possibly, but there's a dark stain on the upper leg, though not very obvious unless you look closely." He pulled the corduroys out of one of his plastic bags.

"You brought them here?" Helen asked. "Not that I should be surprised by anything you do anymore."

"I paid three pounds for them."

"Well, they won't fit me," she said holding the ribbed velour against her leg. "I'm too short. Shame. It's a lovely plum shade."

"I'm going to give them to Inspector Fiske for analysis. See that stain mid-thigh?"

Helen flapped the trousers open so the front was displayed. "Just barely. Mostly in the grooves."

"I didn't notice anything on them when I was speaking to her last night, but by then it was dark outside and the hall was only dimly lit. Not to mention it would have been rude to stare at her legs."

He had noticed Trey's brogues earlier that night, however, having dropped his business card in an attempt to get a close look. These had shown no trace of blood in the decorative perforations in the leather, which would be nigh impossible to clean in a limited amount of time.

Helen brought the corduroy material up to her face. "They've been washed. I can smell lemony detergent or fabric softener. I wonder what brand she uses."

"It didn't get it all out."

"And your suspicious mind is thinking it might be blood."

Rex took the corduroys from her and folded them back up neatly. "It's a good way to hide evidence, donating something to charity among a pile of other clothing. You don't even have to leave a name, and she didn't. Anyhow, I do have something for you that isn't another woman's castoff."

He returned to the car for the roses and held them out to her in the kitchen.

"Oh, Rex, you shouldn't have." Helen took the bouquet and put her nose to them. "Actually, I really don't know why people say that. I'm so glad you did. What's the occasion?"

Remembering his comment to Snyder, he did not want to come up short. "They're for my beautiful wife on our first week wedding anniversary." He hoped she didn't think the roses were a peace offering for bailing out of the packing in the pursuit of a potential murder investigation.

"How sweet. But we're not going to have much time to enjoy them."

"We can take them back to Edinburgh," he said as she lay the flowers on the counter and reached for a vase in the cupboard.

"They'll wilt in the car."

"In that case, we'll leave them for Julie."

While he finished unpacking the bags, Helen filled the vase with water from the sink. "Now, tell me about the rest of your morning. You have that look about you."

"What look?" Rex asked innocently.

"The look of a satisfied cat. A big ginger tom. I sense there's more."

"Och, I'm a long way from catching the canary. But a wee birdie did tell me something of interest."

"I can't wait to hear." Helen placed the flower arrangement on the table, which was set for lunch. "Homemade lentil soup and avocado salad. Will that do you? I thought we could have the leftover curry for dinner." She went to the gas cooker, adjusted a temperature knob, and stirred a wooden spoon in a saucepan.

"Perfect." Rex sat down and shook out his napkin. "Well, as luck would have it, Tony was visiting Penny."

"Progress, indeed!" Helen brought two bowls of soup to the table and took her seat opposite him. "I know you wanted to talk to him."

"Marginal progress on that front." Rex took up his spoon. "To begin with, Tony does not know who was responsible for operating the curtains last night, unless it was Bill."

"For the director, Tony seems curiously uninformed," Helen remarked. "But he's probably more of a creative than practical person, which stands to reason, given his occupation."

"Aye, I can see him teaching art to children," Rex said, adding a sprinkle of rock salt to his soup. "He carefully considers what he's going to say before he speaks. He was a bit reticent to begin with, but did open up gradually. According to Penny, his sister took an overdose of sleeping pills when she was eighteen. Seems Cassie reminded Tony of her, and Penny now says she may have mistaken his innocent affection for Cassie as attraction."

"Oh, dear," Helen said with a worried frown. "I hope she's not getting her hopes up again."

"And then I went to see Rodney Snyder, the man who played Sherlock Holmes."

"Ah, now I get it." Helen gave a knowing smile. "He owns a flower shop, doesn't he? But the roses were still a very thoughtful gift," she added, trying to keep a straight face.

Rex put on a contrite one. "I wanted to get you a little something and I remembered A Rose by Any Other Name."

She laughed into her napkin. "I think a 'whatever' is in order here. Moving on …"

Rex buttered his roll. "Well, Rodney Snyder pretty much confirmed what Tony had told me regarding who was backstage at the time of the shooting. We didn't have a long chat because a customer came into the shop, and he appeared to be working by himself."

"So where does this leave you in the investigation?"

"Good question. Trey Atkins, three of the fictional detectives, the butler, and Tony were backstage at the time of the shooting. The producer had already left to go to his car. Bill and Ben had gone for a smoke. So, too, Robin Busket and the solicitor. Miss Marple, Aunt Clara, and Father Brown were down the hall in the loos." Rex counted them off on his fingers. "If everyone is accounted for at the crucial moment, there must be one unknown person in the mix, unless someone is lying or mistaken. Wouldn't be the first time."

"You are completely ruling out suicide and accidental death, then?"

By this point, the spectre of suicide had all but vanished from Rex's mind, displaced by a yet faceless killer whose motive he could not imagine.

"For now," he replied. "We won't know for sure until the gunshot residue tests come back from the lab. Well, Fiske should know, and hopefully he'll inform me. If none is found on Cassie's hand, the revolver likely didn't go off while she was holding it. The ME said he would call Fiske on Monday with the results of the autopsy. Presumably he's working over the bank holiday. I don't know if the lab is." Rex saw that Helen had put down her spoon. "Perhaps we should change the subject for now. Have you spoken to Julie today?"

"Yes, she rang earlier for an update on the shooting. And to see if we needed any help with the packing."

In Rex's mind, the words Julie and help did not go hand in hand. "And what did you say?"

"I thought she'd only be in the way, especially when she said she could bring the first load of her stuff over. But I invited her over for Sunday lunch."

"You told her she would be in the way?" Rex interjected in surprise. Julie was highly sensitive and had to be treated with kid gloves. No one knew that better than Helen.

"Of course not. That's only what I thought. And I knew what you'd say. So I just said we had everything under control and were hoping to spend some time alone together this afternoon. Unless you have other suspects to visit?" Helen raised her blonde eyebrows at him in enquiry and continued eating her soup.

"I may have run out of suspects to annoy for now. No, I'm all yours."

"Ah, music to my ears," his wife said with a flirty grin. "And I do love the roses," she added, admiring them on the table.

ELEVEN

THE NEXT MORNING, AS Rex and Helen sat at the breakfast table leafing through the Sunday papers for any further news on Cassie Chase's death, the house phone trilled in the hall.

"I wonder who that could be," Helen said with a frown, looking undecided as to whether to answer it. "If it's important and someone I know, they'd call on my mobile." The phone kept ringing and she got up from her chair with a sigh, tightening the belt on her pink satin dressing gown. "It had better not be someone selling double glazing or I'll give them a piece of my mind, ringing at nine a.m. on a holiday weekend!"

Rex smiled. His wife, while being the sweetest person in the world, could make her displeasure sorely felt on rare occasions.

"Helen d'Arcy," he heard her answer in a matter-of-fact tone. "I mean, Mrs. Graves."

Rex chuckled into his mug of coffee. "It's for you," he heard her call out to him. Thinking it might have something to do with the case, he immediately set aside his newspaper and went to join his wife in the hall, where she stood with a hand over the mouthpiece.

"Who is it?" he asked.

"He wouldn't say, but he sounds upset."

Rex took the receiver from her. "How can I help you?" he asked.

"Mr. Graves?" a muffled male voice asked, as though he had been crying.

"Speaking."

"I thought you should know; she did it because of me. I told her I couldn't marry her." The caller broke down in anguish at the other end of the line.

"Are we talking about Cassie? Is this Trey? Calm yourself, lad. I'm having difficulty understanding you. I'm sure you're not responsible. Would it help to talk in person? Perhaps with my wife? Helen is a school counsellor. She's really good in these situations."

Helen, who had returned to the hall with her coffee, gave a concerned nod.

"Thank you," the caller murmured. "But I have to go now."

The phone went dead all of a sudden, and Rex stood listening to the disconnected line. "He rang off," he told Helen in a puzzled tone.

"Remorse?" Helen asked.

"For spurning Cassie? He was in an emotional state on Friday night when I spoke to him, but composed enough. He sounded highly agitated just now and a bit incoherent. I just hope he's not going to do anything stupid."

"Oh, Rex, I hope not! Ring him back."

Rex retrieved the number using the 1471 feature code and pressed "3". The phone rang at the other end, and kept ringing. "I wonder if it's Ada Card's number," he murmured. "I think he's staying with her."

"Hello?" an older male voice answered just then.

"Oh, hello! Could I speak to Trey Atkins?"

"The young man who just left? He got in his car and drove off."

"I'm not sure he should be driving. He's under a lot of stress."

"Seemed all right to me. But I don't know him. I was just passing the pay phone and it was ringing. I felt it would be wrong to ignore it, in case it was urgent."

"Where is the pay phone located?"

"At Morton's Petrol Station at the ring road north of Derby. Is he your son?"

"No, but I have a son his age. I was trying to help him."

"Like I said, he looked okay, but I wasn't that close and he was wearing sunglasses, so I can't be sure."

"Thank you. Can you tell me what he was driving?"

"A Vauxhall Hatchback. Grey, I think, or silver."

Rex thanked the Good Samaritan once again and replaced the receiver. Helen stood leaning against the wall, cradling her mug.

"Should we ring Ada?" she asked. "Penny will have her number. Should I ask for Trey's mobile number as well?"

Rex nodded, seriously concerned about the lad's frame of mind, as was Helen, judging by her expression as she ran upstairs for her mobile phone. He rang Fiske at the station, but was told that neither he nor the sergeant were there. He hesitated to call the inspector at home on a Sunday morning.

He heard Helen talking upstairs and presently she returned with two numbers written on a sheet of notepaper.

"The top one is Ada's home number, but Penny thought she might be at church."

This Rex found was no doubt the case when he tried phoning and received Ada's answering machine. He left a message. His call to Trey's mobile yielded the same result, and he left another brief message asking that he ring back at the earliest opportunity. Of course, it was possible the police had Trey's phone and were scouring it for leads.

This was turning out to be a frustrating morning, Rex decided, and it was concerning he could not get hold of Trey.

"Do you think we should send the police after him?" Helen asked.

"I don't think there's enough justification. We don't know for sure he's suicidal, and he might not appreciate our interference. Plus, he could be miles away from the service station by now."

"So, what do we do now?"

"We wait. Or rather, I think I'll go over to the community centre, take a look around the grounds. There's not likely to be much activity at this hour on a Sunday. Could you hang around in case Trey tries ringing on the land line again?"

"Of course, but let me take a quick shower first."

While Helen went back upstairs, Rex gathered his wallet and the keys to his wife's car. He had left his less roomy Mini Cooper in Edinburgh when they had driven down together on Friday morning. The boxes they were not taking were neatly stacked in the main bedroom and two smaller ones were tucked in the broom closet under the stairs, since Helen did not have a garage. He thought of all the wedding gifts at his mother's house waiting to be sorted. Yet more boxes, he despaired.

"Okay, you can go now," Helen, wrapped in a bath towel, called over the bannister. "I'll be able to hear the phone if it rings."

"All right, lass. What time should I be back for lunch?"

"Julie's coming at eleven. We'll probably eat at twelve thirty."

"Ring me if you need anything. Do we have wine?" Julie liked her white wine.

"I put a bottle in the fridge. Good hunting," Helen added as he opened the front door.

He certainly hoped to catch a nice lead. And there was always a chance Ada, Trey, or Inspector Fiske would return his call while he was out reconnoitring the community centre. In any case, he felt better doing something active, rather than sitting at home waiting. He only had two days left to make some headway in the case.

TWELVE

When Rex reached Hill Grange Community Centre, he saw no other cars in the lot. He parked in one of the marked-up spaces and wandered in the May sunshine towards the two-storey brick building, where he found blue-and-white caution tape girding the entrance.

Following the concrete path to the far corner, he ran into a wiry man in a flat cap and shirtsleeves, and shapeless brown corduroys and work boots.

"And who might you be?" the man asked in a gravelly voice, regarding him suspiciously.

"I'm a private detective. Penny Spencer, whose play was performed on Friday night, asked me to lend assistance in the shooting incident. And whom might I be speaking with?"

"Nob Jensen, the caretaker. A bicycle belonging to one of the actors went missing that evening and I said I'd take a gander while on my rounds."

"Mightn't the police have taken it if they found it on the premises?" Rex asked.

"That's what I told Mr. Holden, him what plays the clergyman. Happens I haven't found so much as a bit of litter, just a new badger's burrow. Right pests they are, tearing up the grass."

"At what time did Mr. Holden last see his bike?"

"He said he arrived sometime before six and noticed it were gone at ten thirty, when he left to go home."

"Were you here on Friday evening?"

"I were round my sister-in-law's. But I were in the hall that afternoon until four setting out the chairs."

"Did you go backstage?"

"No reason to. But I did go back here to check the emergency exit. Mr. Holden lent his bike against that tree and has been known to use this door when leaving after rehearsals, instead of the front entrance. I've told him often enough not to. But it were locked on Friday afternoon when I left."

"There's no fire alarm fitted?"

"Not since the building was a school."

"Why'd he keep his bicycle back here? There's a bike rack out front."

"He didn't have a lock for it and I expect he didn't want it stolen, even though somebody'd have to be desperate to take it, it were such a rusty old heap."

"Is it just yourself who takes care of the community centre?"

"I have two ladies come in midweek to clean the communal areas and offices. I do the stage and back rooms, as there's a lot of stuff lying about what could trip a body up."

"Do the cleaning ladies have keys to the building?"

"No, I always let them in and stay to supervise."

"Who else has keys?"

"I lent one to Mr. Wade, the play's producer, so he could let the cast and crew in for rehearsals. I live on the grounds and come by every morning and again at nine at night to check everything is locked up and in order. They was usually gone by then."

In spite of what Ben Higgins had said about Jensen being "a lazy old git," he seemed to Rex to be efficient enough, and the grass, hedges, and flowering bushes in the grounds looked neatly tended.

"But on opening night, you were at your sister-in-law's house?" Rex clarified.

"I was going to go in later, after the reception, to clean up, but we saw the police cars on our way home. 'What's going on here?' I asked the missus. I thought at first there'd been a bomb scare, and then a bobby told us someone in the play had been shot. I asked who, and he said it were a lass. I knew right then it had to be Cassie. Such a kind and thoughtful girl, she was. Once, when I were locking up, she said, 'Sorry we ran overtime, Mr. Jensen, but I think we left everything nice and tidy for you.' She and the tall young man made a nice couple. I sometimes saw them lingering in the car park by his shiny BMW coupe. I thought, 'He's doing all right for himself. That girl could do a lot worse.' And he was gone on her. You could tell that a mile off. And now this tragedy."

Jensen removed the flat cap from his cropped grey hair and clamped it to his chest. "What a shame! And now I have to get the hall ready for the memorial service," he said with a sad shake of his head.

"It's being held here?" Rex asked in surprise. "When?"

"Four o'clock tomorrow. Ms. Spencer said the police inspector had agreed as long as no one goes near the stage. She asked me to put a platform in front of it for the speeches. No doubt, coppers will be there to make sure no one trespasses. Ms. Spencer and the actors feel the hall is the most appropriate place." Jensen glanced at the redbrick building. "It's where Cassie Chase drew her last breath."

"It's bound to be packed," Rex remarked, fully intending to be there. "By all accounts she was very popular."

"I just hope no one thinks to bring candles. We can't be having those. Too much of a fire hazard, I told Ms. Spencer."

"Thank you, Mr. Jensen. I won't take up more of your time."

The caretaker nodded and pulled his cap back on, continuing along the path to the front entrance, while Rex headed towards the next corner of the building looking for other points of access and egress. Despite what the morning caller had said about being responsible for Cassie's suicide, Rex remained sceptical that she had died by her own hand, and the murderer may well not have used the main entrance.

He found another emergency door exiting from the hall close to the stage. The path ended beyond the two tall windows, and rather than walk on the grass, he returned the way he had come, passing the birch tree that Timothy Holden had used to prop his bicycle against during rehearsals. If the police had not taken the bike into evidence, who had stolen it? Had it simply been a random theft by someone prowling around the community centre on opening night?

As Rex was walking back to his car pondering these questions, the phone jangled in his jacket pocket. A Derby number, he saw when he pulled it out, and he hurried to answer it.

"This is Ada Card," said a brisk voice. "You left me a message to ring you at once."

"Aye, thank you. It was regarding Trey. I wanted to make sure he was all right."

"Better, I think. We just got back from church, otherwise I would have rung sooner."

"Trey was with you at the service?"

"Yes. I suggested he come with me, and it did him the world of good."

Ada had already struck Rex as a do-gooder, but the news of Trey's whereabouts surprised him.

"A local church?" he asked.

"St. Thomas on Pear Tree Road."

Pear Tree, a suburb of modest terraced housing, was located south of the city centre. If Trey had called from a public phone north of Derby less than an hour earlier, he could not have been attending church.

"Ms. Card, what kind of car do you drive?"

"Excuse me?"

"Make and colour of your car?"

"Why on earth?"

"I'm following a lead. As you may have heard, I solve mysteries in my spare time." Rex hoped this would resonate with Ada, whom Trey had mentioned was an Agatha Christie fan. "Inspector Fiske is on board," he added for good measure.

"Well, I don't suppose it's classified information," Ada said loftily. "I own a mustard yellow Mini-Minor, called Mimi."

Rex smiled to himself. "And what does Trey drive?" Jensen had mentioned a BMW coupe.

"A rather nice BMW," Ada replied. "Don't ask me what model, but a newer one. Midnight blue. I really don't understand your line of inquiry, Mr. Graves."

"I just need to confirm where Trey was this morning."

"He spent the whole morning with me. He's a sensitive young man and has been deeply affected by Cassie's death, as you can imagine. They were secretly engaged, you know. I feel it prudent to keep an eye on him in his fragile state. His parents are away in Hong Kong, but his mother is coming home to be with him. Is there anything else?" Ada asked in a manner indicating she wished to terminate the conversation.

"Ehm, yes. If I could just have a quick word with Trey? Thank you again."

"Trey, dear. Rex Graves wants to speak to you," he heard her call out in a neutral tone.

"This is Trey." The voice on the phone was similar to the one Rex had heard earlier, but calmer, less high now in pitch. From their first conversation in the hall, Rex had discerned that the mannerly, well-spoken Trey likely came from a family of means. Aside from which, Hong Kong was not exactly a budget destination.

"How are you bearing up, lad?"

"All right, thank you."

"And how was church?"

"Fine." Trey sounded less enthused than Ada had given herself credit for.

"Do you still have my business card?" Rex enquired.

"It's in my wallet."

"Good. I wasn't sure if you had tried to reach me earlier."

"No, I didn't."

"Well, ring if you feel I might be able to help in any way."

"I shall."

Perplexed, Rex ended the call and unlocked the door of the Renault, but before he could get in, his mobile went off again, and this time it was Inspector Fiske.

"I'm very glad to hear from you," Rex told him. "A few potentially interesting things have come up."

"I'm all ears. I was going to grab a pub lunch. Perhaps we could meet up for a pint?"

"That would be grand, but my wife is preparing Sunday lunch." Rex had an idea. "Why don't you join us? Her friend Julie will be there. Helen is making roast beef and Yorkshire pudding. There'll be plenty to go around, especially since Julie eats like a bird."

"Cheers, I'd like that." Fiske sounded genuinely pleased. "If you're sure…"

"It would be our pleasure." Rex gave the inspector directions to Helen's house.

"Barley Close? I worked a case in that cul-de-sac. An affluent young married couple found dead in their home, while their daughter and her half-brother were asleep … The parents were found by the boy's mother. Yes, I remember now: you turned that case on its head. So, this one will be your third in Derbyshire. Well, we'll have lots to talk about. I can be there in half an hour."

Rex called Helen immediately. "I hope you don't mind, but I've invited Inspector Fiske to lunch."

"Not a problem. We'll just add another place setting. Good idea," she added in a knowing tone. "For both you and Julie."

Rex chuckled. "Are you matchmaking? Julie and Fiske are like chalk and cheese."

"Opposites and all that," Helen said with a hopeful lift in her voice.

Rex heard Julie say something in the background and Helen respond, "We have a surprise guest coming for lunch. Better get back to the pots and pans," she told Rex.

"I'll see you in twenty minutes."

He felt quite pleased with himself. Unlike Helen, he held out no hope in the matchmaking department, but the opportunity to spend some relaxed time with Fiske discussing the case and sharing new information was indeed heaven sent.

THIRTEEN

REX ARRIVED BACK AT Helen's house five minutes before the inspector rang at the door carrying a bottle in a brown paper bag twisted at the neck.

"I stopped by the offie. A Shiraz. I hope it's okay," Fiske said.

Helen stepped into the hall drying her hands on a tea towel. "Perfect. Julie likes white, but I prefer red wine with beef." Tantalizing aromas of roasting meat and potatoes wafted from the kitchen. She gave the bottle to Rex to open. "I thought drinks in the garden first might be nice as it's such a beautiful day, but lunch is just about ready. Perhaps we can have coffee and dessert outside afterwards."

The inspector proffered his crooked smile. "It's nice to see you again under more pleasant circumstances, Helen."

At that moment, Julie made an appearance on the stairs in a short yellow summer dress and wedged espadrille sandals. Evidently, she had been taking advantage of the sunny weather to cultivate a tan. Her hair, which Rex had known in various shades of brown to blonde, was currently as bleached as he had ever seen it. He made the introductions.

"Just Mike," the inspector amended. "Lovely to meet you, Julie."

"Why don't you both go through to the dining room," Helen suggested. "Rex will bring in the wine."

Rex decided to have a Guinness instead, and the inspector opted for one too, saying he was technically on the job and needed to keep his alcohol intake light.

"Well, this is a bit decadent," Helen said with a laugh when they were seated at the oval gateleg table, except for Rex who stood carving the roast at the sideboard. "Here I am with a bottle of red all to myself, while Julie has hers of white!"

"Och, I'll help you finish the red tonight," Rex assured his wife.

"And white keeps for weeks in the fridge," Julie chimed in, smiling at the inspector.

Rex doubted wine lasted that long in Julie's fridge, but kept that thought to himself. He distributed the plates of meat. "Too rare?" he asked Fiske, who had expressed his preference for less well-done beef.

"Not at all. Just pink enough. And Yorkshire pud. Oh, my,"

Helen bid her guests serve themselves to the potatoes, vegetables, and gravy. Bowls were passed around the table, which was decked in a fresh floral-pattern cloth with matching napkins. Rex sat down with his plate.

"Julie teaches geography at my old school," Helen told the inspector in a conversational manner. "Plus, we've known each other for ages."

He took up his fork. "So, you're a fellow teacher of Penny's?" he asked Julie, who nodded. "Do you know her well?"

"Penny's been at Oakleaf Comp less than a year. She was teaching in Paris before that. If I were her, I would have stayed over there. Derby is so boring."

"Well, maybe compared to Paris," Helen conceded.

"Have you been to Paris?" Fiske asked Julie.

She slumped dispiritedly in her chair. "Not since uni. Lucky you, moving to Edinburgh," she said to Helen.

"Julie will be living here and keeping an eye on the house," Helen told the inspector.

"Well, that's a good arrangement. It's a nice place you have here, Helen. This is delicious, by the way. Sunday dinner is one of the things I miss most about being married."

That did not bode well for Julie, who could scarcely boil an egg, Rex could not help but remark to himself.

His wife reached out and touched the inspector's sleeve. "I'm so glad you could come, Mike. Truly. And I'm sure you need a short break from the case."

The inspector dabbed at his mouth with his flowery napkin, which looked incongruous in his large hands. "It has been a bit consuming these past few days. I was seconded to the case due to its sensitive and potentially complex nature. The pressure from the media to solve it is intense." He turned to Julie. "I don't believe I saw you at the community centre on Friday."

"No, I was on a blind date. Horrid waste of time. He was a drummer in a crummy local band and had arms like a gorilla."

Fiske chuckled.

"I did try to warn you," Helen murmured.

Julie tilted her head coquettishly as she looked over at the inspector, her hand fingering the base of her wine glass. "I was supposed to go to the play last night but, naturally, it was called off."

"I was at the community centre this morning when you called," Rex said to Fiske. "More vegetables?" He offered him the tureen of peas and carrots.

"Don't mind if I do." Fiske helped himself and ladled gravy from the white china sauce boat that was part of the dinner service.

"I ran into the caretaker," Rex continued telling the inspector, "and he informed me a bicycle had been stolen on Friday night. Did the police happen to recover one?"

"No. Whose was it?"

"It belongs to Timothy Holden, who plays Father Brown. When he went to retrieve it on Friday night to ride home, it was gone."

Inspector Fiske glanced around the table with a humorously diabolical grin, which was facilitated by his lopsided mouth. "The getaway vehicle?"

"Not sure," Rex replied. "But it is a coincidence it went missing that particular night."

"Indeed," the inspector said.

"Another funny thing," Rex told him. "Helen received what might have been a prank call this morning." He relayed how a sobbing male voice had confided to him that he was the cause of Cassie's suicide for not having wanted to marry her; but that, having spoken with Ada Card and Trey Atkins later that morning, he'd discovered Trey had not been north of Derby, the location of the pay phone from which the call had been placed. Nor had Trey admitted to making the call. "Now, I spoke to him on Friday night and gave him my card with my mobile number on it," Rex added, "so why he would ring Helen's number is peculiar, especially since he doesn't know her. And why use a public phone? Presumably he has a mobile."

"He does, but we have it," the inspector informed him. "We're checking the calls and messages on it. Perhaps he misplaced your card and got Helen's number from a mutual acquaintance, maybe Penny Spencer, so he could get hold of you that way?"

"The caller rang on my landline," Helen told Fiske. "My friends usually call my mobile, which is the number I give out. I don't really know why I've kept the house phone."

"Perhaps he got the number through Directory Enquiries?" the inspector proposed.

Helen shrugged in a way that showed she was unconvinced. "If he knew my surname, which I suppose he could have got from someone. My maiden name, that is. I'd still be under d'Arcy in the book. But if it was Penny, she would have given him my mobile number."

"Perhaps I should check with Penny," the inspector concluded. "And I'd like to speak to Trey to find out why he would pretend not to have rung you, if he did," he said, turning to Rex.

"Unless Ada is covering for him, he could not have made the call from the pay phone," Rex restated. "So, who did? Someone impersonating Trey and trying to throw me off the scent?"

"Which begs the question, why?" Fiske noted.

"Do you think you will get the postmortem results tomorrow?"

"All being well. Dr. Hennessey is highly reliable. Ladies, I hope you don't think me rude for talking shop at table."

"No, you're all right," Helen assured him. "Anyway, it was my incorrigible husband who brought it up." She directed an impish smile at Rex.

"Regardless of who brought it up, we're just as interested as the next person to know what happened to the young actress," pronounced Julie, who was slowly making her way through a meagre meal, having eschewed the Yorkshire pudding as being too stodgy, which meant all the more for Rex. "And Penny wants the case wrapped up quickly."

"She does," the inspector agreed. "As does everybody."

"Did you get the DVD from her?" Rex asked.

"I did, and watched it this morning. Not really my cup of tea, but it was clever of Ms. Spencer to come up with the plot. She is single, is she not?"

"She's got a thing for the play's director," Julie jumped in to answer. "Tony something-Italian. She confided in me one day in the staff room after she thought he'd blown her off."

"I think it might be on again," Rex remarked. "They looked quite cosy yesterday morning at her house."

Julie gasped. "You mean he spent the night?"

"No, I just meant they seemed close, maybe just united in their grief. They weren't holding hands or anything. Tony doesn't seem very expansive for a man with Italian blood in his veins."

"It's probably diluted," Julie said. "Third or fourth generation."

At that moment, the inspector's mobile went off on his person. He read the screen. "Yes, Dan," he said into the phone, and listened for a minute. "Be right there." He looked over at Helen. "Duty calls," he apologized. "A domestic to attend to. Sorry to have to break up the party."

"Do you have time for desert? Julie brought us a treacle tart."

"One of my favourites, but I really can't stay, more's the pity."

"Why don't I find a Tupperware so you can take a piece with you?" Helen suggested, ever practical.

"I wouldn't say no." He smiled at Julie. "And thank you."

"I didn't make it," she confessed with a sheepish grin. "It's from the local bakery."

"I will enjoy it nonetheless," Fiske said gallantly, rising from the table as Helen got up and left the room.

"I almost forgot," Rex told him, following into the hall, where he picked up the bag from Oxfam and handed it to the inspector.

Fiske pulled out the purple corduroys. Rex explained how he had come by them and what he had found on the right leg.

"Yes, I remember Susan Richardson wearing these, and very nice she looked in them, too," Fiske murmured as Julie passed in the hall carrying the wine glasses. "I'll get this stain checked out." He bundled the garment back into the bag and, after accepting the plastic container Helen gave him, bid them all a final goodbye and departed out the front door.

"That went well, I thought," Rex said, returning with his wife to the kitchen. "But he does not seem any further along in the case than I at this point. Unless he's playing things very close to the chest."

"I like him." Helen started loading crockery into the dishwasher. "What did you think?" she asked Julie, who was hand-washing the glasses.

"Quite attractive in a rugged sort of way. Yes, very manly."

"I meant his personality," Helen insisted, with a conspiratorial wink at Rex.

Julie removed the primrose yellow rubber gloves. "Dependable? Courteous. Though I bet he can be quite intimidating when he wants to be." She turned around from the sink. Through the window behind her a cloudless blue sky beckoned. "I thought about giving him my number when he was leaving but lost my nerve. In any case, he's got his hands full right now. If he's interested, he can always get it from Rex."

Julie's voice came across as matter-of-fact, but her narrow face betrayed a hope that the inspector might want to see her again. Although Helen's age, she dressed far younger than her years, and her maturity level was more on a par with the teenagers she schooled in geography. Rex rather wished she might find a good man to take care of her, so she would be less dependent on Helen emotionally. Julie was one of the reasons Helen had delayed making the move to Edinburgh. But he doubted Fiske was the man.

The women decided to change into their swimsuits and have desert on the back patio. Rex, not much of a sunbather, took his treacle tart into the sitting room to ponder his next move in the case.

FOURTEEN

REX REFERRED TO THE burgundy-covered theatre programme, which by now looked much the worse for wear, and made notes in his pad. There were five actors in the play whom he had not had an opportunity to speak with, plus the producer. He decided he had no choice but to ring Penny, otherwise he would be at a standstill.

"Sorry to be bothering you again," he said in his most apologetic voice, "but I need a couple more phone numbers."

"No bother," Penny said. "Did you manage to get hold of Trey and Ada?"

"I did, thank you. I thought, of the actors I haven't yet spoken with, Paul Reddit might be the most cooperative, being in the same line of work as myself."

"Oh, yes, he's a solicitor, isn't he? He was typecast for Mr. Farley in the play. I'll text it to you. Anyone else?"

"Ron Wade might be another logical choice, since you asked him to intercede with the detectives on my behalf."

"Consider it done. How are things progressing?" Penny asked anxiously.

"A few potential leads have come up. In fact, I wanted to ask if anyone had recently asked you for Helen's phone number."

Penny hesitated. "Not that I remember. Why?"

"It's regarding the call we received this morning on Helen's house phone. I assumed at the time it was Trey, but now I'm not so sure."

"An anonymous call? Was it threatening?"

"No, just puzzling."

"A crank call, probably. When there's a—sorry to say—juicy murder or suicide in the news, loonies crawl out of the woodwork wanting to associate themselves with the case out of some sort of pathological attention-seeking."

"That's a perfectly plausible explanation," Rex agreed. "But the person would have had to have known Helen's maiden name to find her through Enquiries."

"Oh," exclaimed Penny suddenly. "I wonder if it might have been one of the boys at school playing a prank."

Rex mentally palmed his forehead. "Of course. They'd all know her as Helen d'Arcy."

Penny laughed softly. "I'm sure they'd still be calling her that if she were staying on at Oakleaf."

"You should be in the business of crime detection, Penny. You do seem to have a knack for it."

"I think I'll just stick to writing about it in my spare time. But if I can be of further help, don't hesitate to ring me."

"I shall. You'll be at the memorial service tomorrow? I believe the caretaker said you were arranging it."

"Yes. Terrible, isn't it? Who could have foreseen it would turn out like this?"

The killer, presumably, Rex thought, but didn't say as much. "Can Helen and I do anything to help?"

"You're already busy with the case and with packing and what-not. There's really not much to do, and we can't get into the building before tomorrow morning as it's still a crime scene. Mr. Jensen and Tony are lending their assistance. And Ada, Bobbi, and Susan. They're preparing tea sandwiches and cake. Rodney is making a large wreath. But don't bring flowers. A lot were left on Friday night."

"Perhaps a condolence card for Cassie's mother?"

"That would be nice. Addressed to her aunt too. We thought about having a basket where cards could be dropped, and donations for the funeral." Penny's voice faltered at this point.

"Absolutely. We'll see you tomorrow."

"Yes. And I'll text you Paul and Ron's numbers directly."

Rex thanked her and terminated the call with a sigh. He could not imagine what a sorrowful holiday weekend Cassie's family must be spending in the aftermath of her death.

Penny duly texted the numbers. He called the producer first, but got a pompous-sounding recorded message stating that if he wasn't answering, it meant he was busy with a client, which Rex thought unlikely on a Sunday, unless Ron Wade conducted business on a golf course. Next port of call was the solicitor, Mr. Reddit, who was much more obliging and told him he was welcome to come along to his office in the city centre, where, with the play being cancelled, he was spending his now vacant Sunday organizing some papers. Rex said he would be there in thirty minutes and took down the address.

He finished his coffee and took his mug and plate to the kitchen. The sound of female laughter entered through the open window above the sink, which let in a warm breeze laced with the faintly exotic scent of honeysuckle. The two women reclined on deck chairs on the grass with a low picnic table between them strewn with magazines and tubes of sunscreen, Julie in a yellow bikini and Helen resplendent in a shimmering blue one-piece.

He slid open the glass door to the patio and announced he was going out for an hour to meet with Paul Reddit, one of the actors in the aborted play.

"Mr. Farley, the Grove family solicitor?" Helen asked.

"Aye, and Mr. Reddit told me he practises family law."

"It was the perfect role for him then."

"Down to the throat-clearing. He did it a couple of times on the phone. Incidentally, Penny suggested our caller this morning might be a pupil at your old school. That would explain how he got your number."

"The little prick should be expelled!" Julie interjected. "I bet you it's Jez Wyatt. He's the class joker. I've had to give him numerous detentions."

"Jeremy is a disruptive element," Helen agreed. "But it's more a case of high spirits with him. He's not a malicious boy. And it's unlikely he knew Cassie. She's seven years older and never attended Oakleaf."

"The caller mentioned something to the effect he never intended to marry her," Rex said. "In fact, wait just a minute; I wrote it down."

He extracted the folded notepad from the pocket of his trousers and stepped onto the patio. "'I thought you should know; she did it because of me. I told her I couldn't marry her.'" He looked up from his notes. "However, Ada told me Trey and Cassie were engaged."

"Their characters were engaged in the play, interestingly enough," Helen remarked. "But maybe Ada doesn't have the latest information. Just because Trey is staying with her doesn't necessarily mean he tells her everything. Secondly, anyone could have made that up about not wanting to marry her. It's not very specific information. I still don't think Jeremy would do that. Maybe another kid at the school, but I hope not. It's in very poor taste."

"I think you're giving Jez Wyatt way too much credit," Julie said, contradicting her friend. "By the time the miscreants reach your office for a bit of counselling they're acting as though butter wouldn't melt in their diabolical little gobs."

"Well, maybe I'll learn more this afternoon." Rex waved his notepad at the two women and turned on his heel to go back into the house.

After locking the front door behind him as a precaution, he made his way along the path to the driveway and got in the Renault. True to his word, he was at Reddit, Hastings & Associates within half an hour of his call to the solicitor, who met him at the door and led him up the creaky stairs of the old beamed building. Though the premises were relatively small, the address was prestigious, and Mr. Reddit occupied an office overlooking the high street.

He bid Rex take a chair across from a large antique partner's desk laden with buff-coloured files, the four walls surrounding it lined with legal reference works and giving off the frowsty odour of an old library. There were no photos anywhere that Rex could see. As far as he knew, Paul Reddit was a bachelor.

"Excuse the mess. Thought I'd do a bit of late spring-cleaning. My niece Bobbi is our administrator, but I prefer to organize things according to my own tried-and-true system." The solicitor cleared his throat and sat down. He was both in mannerism and appearance much like the character he had portrayed, down to the dark suit, although this one was minus a waistcoat and probably not one of his best, instead relegated to weekend work at his law firm when he was not receiving clients.

"Bobbi, as in Roberta Shaw, who played Robin Busket?" Rex asked, simply for confirmation.

"Yes. The dastardly murderer in *Peril at Pinegrove Hall*. Tea?"

"Thank you, no."

Reddit relaxed into his leather swivel chair. "She's my sister's daughter." He cleared his throat once more, in what Rex took to be a verbal tic rather than a cold or an allergy, since it always had the same mildly phlegmy two-note sound, the second lower than the first. "My niece and I share a passion for the theatre. I saw you milling about when we were being questioned by the detective sergeant. Rodney said you were a private detective. The genuine article," the solicitor said with a quick half-smile. "Unlike his Sherlock."

"I hope you don't feel I'm barging in on the investigation."

"Not I. Penny said she had asked Inspector Fiske if you might help. Or rather she asked Ron to ask him. You seemed quite tight with the detective on Friday night."

"My wife and I had him over for lunch today, in fact."

"Well, I had better watch what I say then," Reddit said with another brief smile. "And you're a barrister. I must say, criminal law never much appealed to me. Of course, I'm not suggesting murder is involved in this case. However, would you be investigating a suicide?"

"I would," Rex said carefully, but truthfully. "I've been asked to look into a suicide before, a case in Florida involving a college student. At this point, nothing can be excluded."

"Well, I don't know what to hope for in terms of lesser evils. Suicide would no doubt be worse for Cassie's mother." A catarrhal cough. "No parent wants to believe their child could be that unhappy. An accidental death would be somewhat better. No one at fault but the victim, yet still tragic. A murder investigation would be ongoing. It could become a painfully long ordeal for the mother and aunt. And if it came to a trial, there's always the chance a jury might acquit. *Hur-rum.*"

Rex took in the grey-haired man sitting comfortably behind his solid desk. "If it were a question of murder, what would be your theory, Mr. Reddit?"

"Well, now." The solicitor crossed his arms, revealing the buttoned white cuffs of his shirt. "First of all, I don't deal in theories, only facts. I am not required to have the imagination of a barrister. I can tell you, though, it's not one of us."

"Meaning the actors?"

"Yes. Or the stagehands. Bill may forget to pay his brain bill, as Ben likes to put it, but they are thoroughly decent blokes, the pair of them."

"And the director and producer?" Rex asked.

"Well, now. *Hur-rum.* Tony is a little temperamental; Ron is more in control. Tony worshipped Cassie. I don't know what Ron

116

thought about her or her performance. He never really lets his feelings show. I can't say I like the man particularly, and I'm sure I'm not alone in that sentiment. But we often have to work with people we don't like, don't we? I dislike many of my divorce clients, to be perfectly candid. Having said that, they usually come to me under stressful situations, betrayed by a spouse and feeling vindictive or victimized and not their best selves. *Hur-rum.*"

"Did you see Tony when you came offstage towards the end of Act One?"

"I did, yes. I followed Susan and my niece out of the parlour. Susan played Aunt Clara, in case you're not familiar with all the names. *Hur-rum.* Tony was sitting at the table with some ruled notepaper, working on something or other. I told him we had nailed it. Bobbi and I went to smoke a celebratory cigarette. The first act is always the most nerve-wracking, but the audience was very receptive, which always helps."

"Did you see Trey Atkins?"

"He was in the dressing room when we passed through to the corridor. Bill and Ben joined us for a puff outside some minutes later."

"Where was this?"

"Out the back. I imagine the police collected all our cigarette butts to support our alibis." Reddit smiled.

"You used the fire exit?"

"Indeed. We didn't want to run into spectators and interfere with their suspension of disbelief if they saw us hanging around with our cigs. *Hur-rum.*"

"Did you see a bicycle?"

"Tim's? It was propped against the tree. I think he was too ashamed to leave it in the bike rack by the front entrance. He doesn't have a full-time job."

"What does he do?" Rex asked.

"He works at a sandwich place down the street. The Lunch Counter. I pop in once in a while. That's how he came to get the part of Father Brown. I asked if he thought the owner would mind putting up a poster for the play, and Tim mentioned he was interested in amateur dramatics. When we lost the original Father Brown to bigger and brighter opportunities in Hollywood, I suggested he audition for the part. *Hur-rum*. Father Brown doesn't have many lines, and Tim was fine in the role. An unfortunate underbite, which gives him a rather pugnacious look, but I've never read G. K. Chesterton, so I don't know what his sleuth is really supposed to look like."

"Unassuming, I seem to remember from *The Blue Cross*."

"Well, Tim is that. Nice chap, if a bit quiet."

Rex was always interested in the quiet types. "And you were still outside having a smoke when the shot went off?"

"Yes. *Hur-rum*. We didn't hear about it until we returned for Act Two at seven minutes to eight. I remember checking my watch, not wanting to be late. By this time, Trey had found Cassie dead onstage, and Rodney was on his way to alert us." Reddit rubbed his dark-sleeved upper arms. "It gives me goose bumps just to think about it. Ron came in soon afterwards. He wasn't in a fit state to begin with, suffering as he was from a migraine spell, and so Tony went to notify the audience."

"Right. And what has been your niece's reaction to Cassie's death?" Rex had not been able to observe Bobbi Shaw closely after the fatal shooting. She had been standing with her uncle smoking by the open window in the hall, her face mostly averted, her movements contained, with none of the easy and fluid grace of Cassie.

"She was saddened and dismayed, naturally," Paul Reddit replied, "but not hysterical like Susan. Bobbi is a very stoic and level-headed young woman, qualities her mother doesn't seem to appreciate as much as she might. My sister is very traditional in her values. She'd like Bobbi to marry a nice professional man and start a family, but I suspect my niece is not much into the opposite sex. I'm not sure she has even broached the subject with her mother. *Hur-rum.* I have a female couple in the process of adopting, as a matter of fact. I hope Bobbi sees how open-minded I am."

That Bobbi might be gay did not surprise Rex. In the play, she had convincingly conveyed the marquis' estranged and illegitimate son in disguise.

"Does your niece like horses, Mr. Reddit? I wondered if the riding clothes she wore in the play were her own?"

"I believe so. The jodhpurs and boots, at any rate. Yes, she's a fine horsewoman. Always been dotty about horses."

"Does she hunt too?"

"As a matter of fact, yes. Quite the outdoorsy type is our Bobbi." Reddit cleared his throat and again offered tea.

Rex was about to answer when he felt his phone vibrate in his pocket. "Excuse me," he said, accepting the call and lifting the mobile to his ear. When the caller announced himself as Ron Wade, Rex asked if he could ring him back directly.

He told Reddit he would leave him to his filing and perhaps see him at the memorial service.

"Let me walk you out." The solicitor followed Rex down the stairs, expressing his sorrow at having to return to the community centre for such a mournful event.

"Thank you for your time, Mr. Reddit," Rex said holding out his hand in the hallway. "I truly appreciate it." He spoke sincerely. The solicitor had been more helpful than he probably knew.

FIFTEEN

Rex rang the producer as he sauntered down the nearly deserted Sunday street to the car. Leaning against it, he gazed across the pavement at a closed lighting shop displaying Tiffany lamps and chandeliers in the windowfront while he waited for Ron Wade to answer.

"Thank you for taking my call," Rex said when he finally did.

"I got your message. I can't talk long. My wife and I are going out."

"Just a few quick questions. And thank you for asking Inspector Fiske if I might participate in the case from the side-lines, so to speak."

"It was Penny's idea, really. What can I help you with?"

"I'm mainly concerned at this point with everyone's movements at the time of the shooting and shortly prior. The inspector gave me a brief overview, but I'd like to fill in the details."

He heard Ron sigh abruptly at the other end of the connection. "Well, as soon as the scrim came down for the attic scene, I left my prompting post behind the Chinese screen and went backstage, closely followed by the five sleuths. The other actors had already left the set."

"Whom specifically did you see backstage?"

"As I told the inspector, it was all a bit of a blur. I had a blinding headache coming on, and all I could think about was getting to my car for my pills. I reclined my seat and closed my eyes for a short while."

"Is there anyone who might have seen you leaving the building?" Rex asked.

"There was a young woman in a stripy pullover by the water fountain in the lobby. She was busy on her phone and I don't know if she noticed me. I learnt afterwards she was a reporter. At the time, I remember thinking her bright jumper was hurting my eyes and wondering why she wasn't in the hall watching the play. The ticket attendant was loitering outside by the bushes having a smoke. He may have said something to me. He was still there when I returned from my car at five minutes to eight. I expect he was able to vouch for me to the police. By the time I got backstage, Cassie's body had been found. Everyone was talking at once. I couldn't think straight. I had to sit down in a quiet corner and wait for the medication to finish taking effect."

"Just one more thing, Mr. Wade. Who operated the curtains at the end of the first act?"

"Bill Welsh."

"He said he forgot."

Ron Wade roundly insulted the unreliable stagehand. "Must have been Tony then. He's supposed to direct things onstage."

"It seems it was not him either."

"Well, you got me. But someone did, right? Or we'd all know what bloody happened onstage."

"Exactly so." Rex thanked the producer again.

He stood hesitating by the car. He did not feel ready to go back to Barley Close. Julie would still be there, and for some reason he felt one too many in her presence. Better to leave the two women to enjoy each other's company a while longer, he decided, and for him to make the most of his free time.

The vision of a glass tankard of Guinness floated into his consciousness, as it often did at such moments, and he thought of the Bells, where the stagehands had gone on Friday night. Googling on his phone, he found there was only one pub by that name in Derby, and it was not too far out of his way.

When he got there, however, neither Bill nor Ben were at the bar, which was mostly attended by locals addressing each other with booze-fuelled familiarity, among them a handful of gussied-up women with loud jewellery, shimmery lipstick, and teased-out hair, laughing raucously.

"What you having, cock?" asked the barman.

Appropriating a table by the window, Rex drank his solitary pint in the cheerless surroundings and thought the case through.

Upon returning to Barley Close an hour later, he saw that Julie's battered red Triumph Spitfire was still parked at the kerb. He briefly wondered how she intended to move all her stuff over in the tiny two-seater, unless she planned to do so in instalments. He found her and his wife finishing a cup of tea in the kitchen, having changed out of their swimwear and back into their summer dresses.

"I'll leave you two love birds to it," Julie announced, rising from the table. "See you Tuesday, if my mum doesn't boot me out before then."

"Not going well at your mother's?" Rex enquired.

"Hardly. It's not easy, living back at home at my age."

"I still live at home," Rex said with a smile.

"That's different. You have a big house and a live-in housekeeper. I'm expected to 'pull my weight,'" Julie mimicked. "Not that Dad pulls his. And then I have to listen to Mum giving me advice, like I was still fifteen years old. I even have a curfew, for Gawd's sake."

Helen laughed. "Don't exaggerate, Julie. Your mother just worries about you. Fifty or fifteen, you're still her only daughter."

"Well, I can't wait to be independent again. I'll love living here. And don't worry, Hells, I'll take the best care of your little house."

"I know you will."

The women kissed on the cheek and Julie gave Rex a quick hug. Helen saw her to the front door, and when she returned to the kitchen, Rex took her in his arms. "I finally have you all to myself," he murmured into her abundant blonde hair.

"You smell of the pub," she said. "Beer, a hint of cigarette smoke, and cheap perfume."

"Guilty as charged," he confessed. "But just to the first."

SIXTEEN

THE AFTERNOON OF THE memorial service turned out as sunny as the preceding day, and while Helen attended to chores inside the house after lunch, Rex undertook the mowing of the modest front and back lawns with her electric push-mower, enjoying the exercise and the scent of warm, cut grass. He hoped Julie would not forget to water the garden when she was living here. After he had finished, he went inside to shower and change, planning to be at the community centre in good time for the service.

When he and Helen arrived, a radio van advertising an oldies station that broadcast to the Midlands was already idling outside the building, its gold-on-black lettering glinting in the bright rays of sun.

"Must be the station Ben works for as a sound engineer," Rex remarked. "Hopefully, there'll be some upbeat music." He was prone to tears at young people's memorial services, and was dreading this one. He eased the car into a space under a spreading horse chestnut tree in full bloom, its candles of white flowers thrust out as though in prayer.

A marked police car lurked in a far corner of the expanse of worn asphalt divided into faded white lines. Rex predicted the Derbyshire detectives would be arriving shortly, if they were not here already. "There's Mike and his sergeant by the entrance," he said, suddenly spotting them.

Inspector Fiske wore a creased jacket and a black tie, while Antonescu was buttoned into a cobalt blue suit that looked tailor-made for his taut and muscular frame.

"I'll go over and have a word."

"I'll see if Penny needs any help." His wife's ex-colleague had just stepped out of her car and was reaching into the back seat for what appeared to be supplies for the service.

"Good turnout," the inspector commented to Rex while his sergeant split off to follow a stream of mourners into the building. "By the way, I really enjoyed lunch yesterday. Helen's a lovely lady."

"Everyone likes Helen," Rex said fondly. "She's steady and understanding, as well as fun. My son adores her."

"She'd make a good copper's wife. The flighty ones can't hack the long hours and unpredictability of the job. I've had more than one wife complain I was married to the force."

Rex nodded in sympathy, privately thinking Julie would not make for a suitable candidate. Conversely, would she really want to be wife number four? "Any news yet on the postmortem?" he asked.

The two men automatically moved away from the glass doors, which had been propped open to accommodate those who had come to pay Cassie Chase their final respects.

"Yes, Dr. Hennessey was true to his word. His report so far shows that Cassie was not under the influence of alcohol or drugs, either prescription or recreational. A four-five-five cartridge, compatible with the Webley revolver found lying beside her, was lodged in her body, having caused a lot of internal damage. A ballistics test will no doubt further prove it was discharged from the Webley, which Trey Atkins claims was still giving off a chemically smoky smell when he found her. It had only her prints on it, but there was not enough GSR on her hand to be able to conclusively rule her death either a suicide or a self-inflicted accident."

"The gunshot residue could have been transferred by the killer placing the revolver in her hand to get her fingerprints on it," Rex suggested as they sauntered along the path skirting the old brick building.

The inspector stopped at the corner and nodded towards a copse of birch trees at the far end of the grounds. "We found a latex glove in the adjacent playing fields, but it was too degraded after the rain early on Saturday and by players' cleats churning it into the mud to render any viable gunshot residue or DNA."

"Anything otherwise telling about the glove?"

"Not really. It was of the close-fitting variety worn by hospital workers and food handlers."

That could apply to at least two members of the cast, Rex mused even as the inspector made the point that the article might have nothing to do with the case whatsoever.

"Can you trace the Webley?"

Fiske gave a dispirited sigh. "It's a mark and model widely used by the British forces in the First and Second World Wars, and popular with collectors. And the six-digit serial number has been filed off."

"Any unaccounted-for shoe prints onstage?" Rex asked in desperation, to which the inspector shook his head once again. "And if I might push further ... was anything discovered at Cassie's home to denote her state of mind?"

"Nothing sinister," Fiske replied, resuming their walk back the way they had come. "Her room was neat and tidy. Soft furnishings in mauve, childhood dolls on display on a shelf. No suicide note, and nothing untoward on her laptop. No postings on social media beyond references to the play and how thrilled she was to be the leading lady, and how wonderful all the actors were; that sort of thing. Trey Atkins isn't on Facebook, so we have less on him. Cassie had lost her mobile phone the day prior to her death, unfortunately, but we have Trey's."

Rex stopped and stood for a moment contemplating the concrete path at his feet, where a single weed had pushed through a crack, and took stock. No definitive proof that the gun had been discharged from Cassie's hand. And no mind-altering substances found in her system, suggesting she had not felt the need to escape the realities of her life, which by all accounts was going well, aside from her mother's illness.

"Any indication in the messages between Cassie and Trey that the romance was waning?"

"On the contrary, it seemed to be going great guns. Forgive the unfortunate pun. A sweet romance, nothing hot and heavy. She was saving herself for marriage. It looked like these two were in it for the long haul. He proposed to her a week ago and corroborated this in his interview with us at the station, but they were keeping it under wraps for the time being."

"Perhaps they were going to announce it after the final performance of the play. A grand finale sort of thing."

"That would be my guess. In any case, she was wearing a ruby engagement ring on a chain around her neck, hidden under her blouse, when she died. Trey confirmed it was the one he had given her."

By this point in the conversation, the two men had wandered back to the entrance, and the inspector excused himself and went into the building.

The car park was filling up with vehicles, and groups of people stood about talking, in a few cases laughing. Only the sombre and, for the most part, formal code of dress gave away the occasion. Rex felt he was appropriately attired in a charcoal-grey suit and navy blue tie, picked out by Helen. He pushed back the cuff of his shirt and glanced at his watch. Fifteen minutes to go before the service was due to begin.

As he looked up, his wife and Penny appeared from the direction of the car park, carrying a small white box and a plastic bag, respectively.

He stepped forward. "Can I lend a hand?"

"This is the last of the paper napkins and plastic forks," Penny replied. "I'm having reservations about the napkins," she told Helen. "Do you think the monochrome is too, well, depressing? I just thought in view of the occasion …" She looked down at her black dress, the same one she had worn on opening night. "Which reminds me, Rex. There's something I wanted to tell you. I mentioned it to Helen and she thought it might be important."

"Here," Helen told Penny. "Let me take the bag. I'll get this lot inside while you talk to Rex."

"I'm all ears," he said as his wife left them. "Did you mention whatever it is to Inspector Fiske?"

"Not yet. You can judge how important it is first."

They stood aside to let pass a throng of people of around Cassie's age.

"Well," Penny began. "On Friday afternoon as I was passing by here in my car, I saw Timothy Holden approach the building in his Father Brown costume, which struck me as odd at the time. That and the fact it was not even five o'clock, too early for the actors to be turning up, even for opening night. The play didn't start until seven."

"Before five o'clock… You're sure of the time?"

"Quite sure, because I looked at the dashboard clock and checked my watch, worried it might be later and I would not get to the dry-cleaner's before it closed, and I needed this dress to wear that night. Timothy was not on his bicycle, but since he was wearing his cassock, I thought maybe someone had dropped him off—although the actors usually change in the dressing room. In any case, I was in a hurry and didn't give it another thought until I heard that his bike had been stolen that night. So, maybe he did come on his bike after all, and went off somewhere on foot for some reason." Penny gazed up at Rex with a quizzical expression.

"Is there a shop close by? Perhaps he went to buy sweets or cigarettes."

"In his cassock?" Penny frowned in doubt. "There is a corner shop about half a mile from the playing fields, the direction he was coming from."

Rex had driven through the neighbourhood and seen turbans and tunics, and women in saris and scarves, along with several teens in slogan tee-shirts and low-riding jeans. He concurred with Penny's scepticism. A man in an old-fashioned clergyman's costume might attract a few curious glances. He made a mental note to ask at the shop if they had served such a customer.

"Anyway," Penny said, "Timothy doesn't smoke and he's on a diet. Hence the bike. That's what he told us, anyway. And I made sure there was always a stock of biscuits and drinks backstage. Most of the actors would come to rehearsals straight from work. Sometimes Cassie brought bran and honey muffins from the bakery." A sad, reminiscing smile came to Penny's lips. She sighed. "I only remembered the incident this afternoon when I was putting on this dress again."

Rex resolved to talk to Timothy Holden and get to the bottom of the subject of the bike, which the caretaker had told him had disappeared between shortly before six and ten thirty on the night of the shooting; and not before five. Why would the actor lie to the caretaker? However, it would have to wait, since Helen came out just then and notified him and Penny that the memorial service was about to begin. Rex braced himself.

SEVENTEEN

THE HALL WAS PACKED to capacity. Rex took a seat with Helen in the last row of chairs, while the two detectives stood at the back, trying unsuccessfully to appear unobtrusive. Antonescu looked more like a bodyguard than a policeman, his obsidian eyes glowering beneath jet-black brows and taking everything in, his facial muscles set in stone. The bereaved family members occupied the front row, along with the cast and crew. Ada Card had saved a place for Penny, waving to her in agitation as the playwright had entered the hall.

A female soprano's voice filled the hall. Sarah Brightman's, according to the reverse side of the gilt-edged memory card in Rex's hand, distributed at the doors. The front showed a thumbnail photo of Cassie, the narrow dates of her birth and death, and a poetical epitaph, which he did not recognize. In front of the stage to the left, a white garland of lilies and roses was displayed beneath a blown-up publicity shot of the deceased girl, smiling amid her wavy, reddish-gold locks. Next to it, wooden pallets had been set side by side, on which stood a lectern fitted with a microphone.

Ron Wade, a pale redhead with a large, flaccid build, had assumed the role of master of ceremonies. He opened his remarks by reflecting that Cassie would not have wanted this day to be a sad remembrance of her, but rather a coming together of those she held dearest, and her profound wish would have been to inspire everyone present to reach for their dreams. Sobs arose from among the attendees. He added that he, for his part, had found her to be an indispensable asset in *Peril at Pinegrove Hall*, where she had proved to be a selfless team player. Rex inwardly groaned; Ron Wade sounded as though he were in one of his sales meetings. He then announced that Cassie's aunt, Belinda Stokes, would now come up and speak.

A trim woman with a youthful face and silvery hair to the shoulders of her loose-fitting, dark purple dress approached the platform and took Ron's place behind the lectern, adjusting the mic stand to her shorter stature. In a steady voice, she talked about her niece's talent, her devotion to her disabled mother, and her cheerful and giving nature.

One by one, friends, coworkers, and fellow actors followed to further praise Cassie's optimistic disposition and generous soul, and to cite anecdotes. It transpired that she had volunteered at an animal shelter before her mother was diagnosed with MS, and had donated buns and loaves of bread to the homeless from the Ceres Bakery she managed.

Bowing over the mic in a narrow black suit that accentuated his spindly height, Christopher Ells, the butler in the play, mumbled a few words, most of which Rex could not hear from the back of the hall. In the intervening distance, his face appeared as a blank canvas punctuated by two dark holes and crowned with a mop of grey hair.

Trey Atkins went up next with Ada Card and blurted out how Cassie had been the light of his life. He got no further, his voice breaking down in despair. Ada smoothly took over and said Cassie would be sorely missed by all who knew her. She was an absolute angel and would look down on them all from heaven. Ben Higgins, dressed in a white shirt and pressed trousers for the occasion, characterized the actress as "a delightful girl and a kind spirit, who never had a harsh word to say about anybody."

Rex knew the detectives would be watching carefully as the cast and crew of *Peril at Pinegrove Hall* gave their speeches. Rodney Snyder went up to the mic and relayed what a joy and privilege it had been to work with Cassie, and then Penny took her turn, tearfully conveying how the young actress had brought her play to life; an unfortunate turn of phrase under the circumstances, Rex thought as he contemplated the deceased's picture looming beside her. Bobbi Shaw, he noted, was conspicuous by her absence. All the other actors in the play, save Tony, sitting beside Penny with his head bowed, had stepped onto the podium and expressed their sentiments.

Poems were recited, including the first four stanzas of Tennyson's *The Lady of Shalott*, which drew more sobs, but whose significance other than the description of a peaceful pastoral setting was lost on Rex. He remembered best from school the third part of the ballad concerning a mirror cracking from side to side and the curse that is brought about after the sequestered maiden first beholds Sir Lancelot upon his fine steed.

"Time to Say Goodbye," a Sarah Brightman duet with Italian tenor Andrea Bocelli, began to play from the speakers. Ron Wade returned to the makeshift podium to wrap up the service and announced that refreshments would be available at the back of the hall. Rex went to avail himself and Helen of a cup of tea, served from a commercial-size metal urn.

As he was returning to their seats, Cassie's aunt wheeled the deceased's weeping mother out through the doors. A handsome redhead, it was clear even in her sitting position that she was tall like her daughter. Evidently, she had not found the strength to speak at the service. Around the hall, groupings of mourners talked in subdued voices.

"Hello, Mr. Snyder." Rex addressed the florist passing in the aisle. "That was a nice eulogy you gave."

"Mr. Graves. Homing in on the killer yet? I heard the police were leaning more towards murder now."

Rex wondered where the man had come by that information. The manner of Cassie's death was still open, as reported by Inspector Fiske. "Any ideas yourself?"

"Someone with a flair for the dramatic," Rodney Snyder replied. "Anyone connected with the play, in fact. I'd be looking at a Shakespearean motive for murder, myself. Jealousy, perhaps." He turned towards the blown-up photo of Cassie at the front of the hall. "She had youth, beauty, and talent. And Trey." He tapped the side of his nose twice. "*Cherchez la femme*," he whispered theatrically, and with an ironic smile went to join Andrew Forsythe, who was attired in a three-piece, dove-grey suit and leaning nonchalantly on his antique cane.

"A bit of a character, that one," Inspector Fiske said, joining Rex and gazing after Snyder. "But then, these people take their craft very seriously, and you never know if they're acting or not."

"Mr. Forsythe is a case in point," Rex agreed. "I think he believes he is indeed Peter Wimsey."

"Did Lord Peter ever actually shoot anyone?"

"I'm not the person to ask. But Rodney Snyder suggested we look for a woman."

"Did he now ... Based on what?"

"He didn't say. He just seems to think jealousy was a motive. Incidentally, did you find blood on the purple corduroys?"

"We did, but we don't know whose yet."

"I noticed a pair of glasses in the dressing room cubicle Susan Richardson used, and which she said didn't belong to her. I got the impression from what she told me that they weren't there when she changed into her costume."

"No one claimed them. We took them in for analysis. They're non-prescription, so probably come from the theatre props." Fiske turned to the back wall, where Trey sat hunched over his memory card, one hand shielding his face, an untouched cup of tea on the chair beside him. "Could that young man inspire the sort of passion to kill oneself over? Seems to me to be a bit lacking in the backbone department."

"Possibly," Rex said, thinking it would be better to have had murder confirmed outright. Then the police could focus on finding the killer.

"I was hoping we'd hear a few more words from him, but apparently, he was too overwhelmed by grief. Even Ells managed a short speech, and he's been the most reticent of the witnesses. Right, well, us cops don't want to outstay our welcome. Perhaps you'll hear something useful, if you haven't already?"

"Not sure how useful yet, but I'll let you know if something comes of it."

Fiske nodded his appreciation and signalled to his sergeant that it was time to leave by pointing to the exit. Rex, still holding his two cups of tea, went in search of Helen and found her with Penny.

"It's probably tepid by now," he apologized, handing Helen her tea and offering Penny his, which she accepted.

"I saw you got waylaid by Mike," Helen said.

"He took off. Did you speak to him?"

"Just briefly. He thanked me for lunch yesterday."

Penny told Rex she had not had the opportunity to tell the inspector about Timothy arriving so early on Friday, but would call him when she got home. Rex asked if she knew why Bobbi Shaw hadn't attended the service.

"Paul said she had a sore throat and had to stay at home in case it was contagious."

"That's a shame. How did your killer in the play interact with Cassie?"

"She acted like a big galumphing puppy around her. Bobbi liked to horse about. It provided some light relief at rehearsals, especially when Lady Naomi's ghost places the footstool in front of her to force her character to reveal the jewels. For the actual performance, it was a challenge not to have the tripping-up scene look too comedic and slapstick." Penny gave him a pointed look. "Why do you ask?"

"I wondered if anybody might have been jealous enough to—"

"Mind if I butt in?"

"Mr. Caldwell, isn't it?" Rex addressed the short newcomer.

The actor was almost unrecognizable as Poirot, and certainly didn't sound like the Belgian detective, being from Derbyshire. "Lovely service, Penny," he praised her.

"Thank you, but I had a lot of help."

"Do you know what the Tennyson reference was about?" Rex asked them. "I'm afraid it was a bit lost on me."

"Cassie first acted with Trey in a rendering of *The Lady of Shalott*, where they played the leads," Dennis Caldwell explained. "The girl who read the opening verses was Cassie's understudy. I played one of the guards. We were all dressed in medieval costume."

"It was very movingly read by that young woman," Helen remarked, looking in the direction of a brunette holding a chubby baby and talking to two men of her age.

Caldwell nodded. "It certainly put a lump in my throat."

"You are very active in community theatre, Mr. Caldwell?" Rex enquired.

"It's a good way to make contacts. I'm in the insurance business." He produced a card from his suit jacket. "I insured Cassie, as a matter of fact. Stroke of luck, really, for her mum."

"I'm not sure I would put it quite that way," Rex objected mildly.

"Well, obviously. But one has to be pragmatic in my line of work. I had put it to Mrs. Chase that, as her daughter was her primary caregiver, it might be prudent to take out a policy, just in case. So now, at least, Mum gets a substantial enough sum to retain the services of a nurse's aide. And double the amount if Cassie's death is ruled accidental or foul play," Caldwell added in a self-congratulatory tone, while Helen and Penny quietly excused themselves and slipped away towards the refreshments. "It's too much work for Cassie's aunt to take on, on her own."

"I imagine it is," Rex agreed, his heart going out to Mrs. Chase, forced to deal with such practicalities before her daughter was even buried. "And in the event of suicide?"

"No payout. But I doubt it was suicide. Do you have any children, Mr. Graves?"

"A son, grown."

"Any kids on your new wife's side?"

"No," Rex said with a sad shake of his head, knowing how much Helen regretted not having children of her own, and how much she would miss her favourites at her old school.

"Life is unpredictable," the insurance salesman opined with a sigh. "Always best to prepare for the worst, I tell my clients. I have a dentist who contracted MS. Can't practise since his hands started trembling, but he had the foresight to insure against misfortune, and now he can still enjoy good quality of life."

"Ehm, I hear you," Rex said vaguely, casting about for an exit strategy. He felt sure Dennis Caldwell would try to sell him a policy. At that moment, Paul Reddit came unwittingly or intentionally to his aid.

"Sorry to hear your niece got taken ill," Rex said, sorry, too, not to be able to speak with her.

"Bobbi is rather susceptible to sore throats. Not a good thing for an actress. She looks as strong as an ox, but there we are. It's due to stress, I think. *Hur-rum.* It was a very nice service, don't you agree, Dennis?" The solicitor addressed Caldwell. "A fitting tribute to Cassie."

"Mr. Caldwell was telling me that she and Trey first met on the set of *The Lady of Shalott*," Rex offered.

"Not sure they hadn't met before." Dennis Caldwell was quick to correct Rex. "But first time acting together. Susan Richardson was his leading lady in a previous production."

"That's right," Reddit stated. "Susan played opposite him in a musical production of *Goodbye, Mrs. Robinson*. Early last year, wasn't it?"

"She was very convincing as a cougar. She's forty-five," Caldwell murmured conspiratorially, "but looks amazingly good for her age. Trey is twenty-six or twenty-seven. I heard she came on to him at rehearsals. The poor lad was too polite to rebuff her advances too brusquely. Then, at the cast party everyone got a bit tipsy, and Susan made a fool of herself, bursting into tears because the show was over."

Reddit glanced at Rex. "Theatre gossip," he muttered disapprovingly.

Rex rather relished gossip when a murder might be involved. "But Trey and Cassie were not going out at that point?"

"So you know about that, do you?" Caldwell asked, raising one of his almost non-existent eyebrows, which had been shaved off and pencilled in for his role as Poirot. "No, Cassie was seeing someone else in theatre. *Peril at Pinegrove Hall* is what brought her and Trey closer together, by all accounts."

"By whose accounts?" Reddit contested. "More gossip and rumour," he told Rex, who turned back to Caldwell.

"Any tension when Trey and Susan found themselves in another production together?" he asked.

"None that I noticed, but I didn't hear about Susan's crush on Trey until this weekend."

"When everyone has been speculating as to motive in the case," Rex said, nodding his head thoughtfully and wondering if Susan Richardson was "the woman" whom Snyder had been alluding to a short while ago.

The only other women in the play were Ada Card and Paul Reddit's niece, neither of whom were serious contenders for Trey's romantic affection, one too old, the other apparently not interested in men. However, could Bobbi have been interested in Cassie, as indicated by the immature behaviour Penny had described? Only, she wasn't available for comment.

Her uncle had moved away to shake someone's hand and exchange sober words about the service, and Rex left Dennis Caldwell to get himself some tea. Just then he spotted Susan, her tall frame clothed in a bottle-green chiffon dress, her dark hair, minus grey streaks, coiled down her bare back. A striking woman, he had reflected upon watching her on the podium. He could not remember much of what she had said; by the time her turn had come, all the words spoken about Cassie had begun to blur. She was now in the company of a balding, strapping man of middle years, whom Rex took to be her husband, and a girl in her late teens, presumably the daughter who attended Oakleaf Comprehensive.

Rex noted that Susan Richardson and Penny Spencer were not dissimilar in terms of age and looks, both dressed with understated elegance. The French teacher stood in a small group by the opulent wreath of white flowers, Tony by her side.

"A Penny for them," Helen said with emphasis on the name, approaching him and following his gaze.

"I was thinking how alike she and Susan are."

"In appearance, maybe, but Penny is a single working woman and Susan is a mother of three."

"What does her husband do?"

"He owns a glass manufacturing business. Custom windows, I think. He travels a lot, she told me. What do you have percolating in that head of yours, Rex?"

He smiled at her amused expression. "Excuse my execrable accent, but *cherchez la femme* does mean 'look for the woman,' correct?"

"Literally, yes. Why?"

"It was something Rodney Snyder said."

"That man is a bit of a snake," Helen remarked under her breath, glancing in his direction. "I was complimenting him on his beautiful wreath and he started plying me for information about your investigative methods."

"And what did you tell him?"

"I said your methods were inscrutable."

"Ah, excuse me one moment," Rex said, having spied Timothy Holden across the hall.

"Where are you going now?"

"*Chercher la bicyclette,*" he answered enigmatically as he sought his next suspect.

EIGHTEEN

"Any luck finding your bicycle?" Rex asked Timothy Holden, who was standing at the back of the hall finishing off a piece of layered sponge cake.

"Nah, gone for a burton," he replied, wiping cream from his mouth with one of Penny's paper napkins. The pronounced underbite and thick lenses magnifying his eyes gave him the look of an insect, further enhanced by the greying brown hair, spare and bristly, cut close to his head. A moth, Rex decided.

"Did you report it stolen?"

Holden's frown deepened. "Not worth it. It's a piece of junk. I just asked Jensen to keep an eye out in case it turned up, but it's prob'ly been cannibalized for parts by now."

"The caretaker said it went missing sometime on Friday evening."

"Why you asking?" Holden, maintaining his perpetually puzzled expression, proceeded to lick his fingers. "Have you tried Ada's cake?" Red jam filling had dribbled onto his wide, brown suede tie, worn over a pastel blue rayon shirt.

"Not yet. You have jam on your tie. Allow me." Rex took the napkin and dabbed the raspberry off as best he could. "As you may have heard, I'm working on the case, but privately. There, that's better." He handed back the napkin, which Holden stuffed into the black, beltless trousers nipping into his expansive waist.

"You're not required to speak to me if you choose not to," Rex said. "I simply wanted to know what time you got here on Friday afternoon. I'm trying to create a timeline."

"Five forty, it was, or thereabouts."

This roughly coincided with what Holden had told the caretaker, and yet Penny had been sure she had seen him approaching the building on foot almost an hour earlier. "And you came on your bike?"

"Right. I don't have a car. I went in early to rehearse before the others arrived. I hadn't had the part very long and was nervous I'd forget my lines. I can't always hear Ron when he's prompting."

"I watched the entire play on DVD. Father Brown doesn't have many lines."

"True, but my memory's not that fantastic. I really can't fathom how actors manage to remember reams of script. I had trouble at school reciting from memory just one verse of poetry. Added to which, I had to do an Essex accent. Rodney helped with that as he's from Essex, same as Father Brown."

"Those setbacks didn't prevent you from taking on the role," Rex pointed out with an encouraging smile.

"Oh, I've always loved the theatre, and Mr. Reddit asked me as a favour, like."

"How did you get into the building?"

"Ron dropped the key off at my work. His office is close by, same as Mr. Reddit's. Said he might be running late from a meeting, but he'd get there by six thirty, so I was to unlock the front door for the rest of the cast."

"Did you change here?"

Holden gave a snorting laugh. "Well, yeah. I could hardly bike in my bleeding costume, now could I? It's like a dress. Imagine the stares I'd get!"

"It would certainly draw some attention," Rex agreed, sharing in Holden's amusement. "So, you arrived at twenty to six, and then what did you do?"

"I parked the bike around the side, same as I always do. Did," Holden corrected himself. "I let myself in the front entrance and went to change. Then I went through my lines onstage. Tony had taped out my marks for me."

"Were the theatre curtains closed?"

Holden nodded and glanced towards them. "And it was quite dark. I could just make out the crosses."

"And you never left the building?"

"Not until I went home that night."

"Who was the next person to arrive, and when?"

"Tony, at around six. The actors began coming in ten minutes later."

"Did anything unusual happen that you can remember?"

"Not until the shooting. I was in the lav when I heard the shot go off."

"You heard it, even though your hearing is impaired?"

"It's not that bad. I have trouble hearing whispers, like when Ron prompts. But I heard the bang through the wall. I wondered what it was, but I wasn't alarmed, exactly. Ada and Susan caught up with me in the corridor. They'd heard it too. When we got backstage we found out Cassie'd been shot. Mr. Reddit, his niece, and the stagehands, they came in a few minutes after us. We none of us could believe it. I still can't."

"Any ideas how it might have happened?"

Holden blinked behind the lenses of his glasses. "How should I know? I wasn't there, was I? You should ask them as were."

"I have. At least most of them. How well do you know Christopher Ells?"

"Better than the others. He's single, same as me, so we hang out in our free time. He gave me a lift here this afternoon, since I'm without transportation."

"What exactly is it that Ells does at the hospital?"

"He works in a pathology lab, cleaning tubes and instruments. Says there's a special kind of oven to sterilize the equipment in. An autoclave, or something."

"And how do you get on with the others?"

Holden gave a small shrug. "Ben and Bill are okay. They mostly stick together. Mr. Reddit is a nice man, but he's a solicitor. Not stuck up, though, not like Rodney or Andrew, who's a bit of a poser. I don't know Dennis Caldwell that well, but I'd never buy a policy off him, and I don't really know the women well, neither. Women tend to ignore me. Not Cassie, though."

"And Trey Atkins?"

"He's all right. A quiet, serious sort of lad. I heard today they'd got engaged. Makes her death that much worse, if you know what I mean."

"I do."

"Look, if you don't mind, I'm going to get some more food. Talking always gives me the munchies."

"By all means." Rex watched as Holden went over to a table and piled a paper plate with salmon paste sandwiches.

Rex looked about the hall and through the open double doors to the lobby, where a few of the mourners had migrated. Others stood outside the building's entrance, taking advantage of the fine evening. He would have liked to talk to Ells, but he was nowhere in sight. Had he left without Holden? Apparently, Holden was wondering the same thing as he meandered about with his laden plate.

Through the forest of people still occupying the space between the double doors and the tables of refreshments, which Ada Card was beginning to clear with a handful of volunteers, Rex spotted Trey standing alone. He made a beeline for him while Ada was occupied, and was greeted by a wan smile of recognition.

"How are you bearing up, lad?"

"So-so." Trey paused and looked at him through tired hazel eyes. "Inspector Fiske asked if I had rung you yesterday. I wondered what that was about."

"I got a call from someone I thought might be you. He didn't give a name, simply implied he was responsible for Cassie's suicide."

"Suicide?" Trey asked in shock. "Responsible how?"

"For refusing to marry her."

"That's nonsense," Trey exclaimed, his face taking on more colour. "Why would I have broken off our engagement?" He looked for a moment as though he might cry bitter tears, and then he stared at Rex. "She wasn't seeing anyone else."

Rex thought he glimpsed just a shadow of doubt. "I've pretty much concluded it was a prank call, possibly from a pupil at Penny's school."

Trey's face tensed up, anger replacing consternation. "I'll thrash him! Who is he?"

"We don't know, but Penny will look into it. Are you still at Ada's?"

"No, I'm headed to Little Eaton to collect my sister from her friend's. We'll be staying at my parents' house. My mother is flying back from a business trip. I really should get going."

"Trey, you seen Chris?" Holden asked, approaching them, having rid himself of his plate and holding a half-eaten chocolate wafer. In the background, the caretaker was going around the hall removing debris left on chairs and disposing of the items in a large black plastic bag.

"Chris Ells? I don't think so. Do you need a lift home? I'm leaving right now."

"Nice one." Holden turned to Rex. "Let me know if you find my bike, ta. You can get my number through Penny."

Trey called out to Ada and waved in farewell, and he and Holden left. Rex could not help but feel that the young man had used the excuse of his sister to make a quick exit. He tailed the two men from a distance and, standing by Helen's car beneath the chestnut tree, watched as a shiny blue BMW turned out of the gateposts. More vehicles followed as the community centre began to clear out in waves. Andrew Forsythe, top hat and cane in hand, walked out arm in arm with a woman in lilac silk tulle and a matching hat, an outfit more appropriate for a garden party, in Rex's opinion. They certainly made a flamboyant pair. Forsythe's wife, if such she was, had apparently recovered from whatever ailment had prevented her from attending opening night.

"Thinking of leaving without me?" Helen asked behind him, giving him a start. "You keep disappearing."

A flood of people poured into the car park at that moment, among them Tony, who left in his old red estate car.

Rex leant against the front passenger door of his wife's Renault. "I wasn't thinking of leaving at all, but I'm running out of people to interview. Trey Atkins had to collect his sister in Little Eaton, wherever that is."

"It's a village northeast of Derby."

Rex fixed his eyes on her. "Would the petrol station we received the call from yesterday be on the way to Little Eaton, by any chance? The man said it was on the ring road north of the city." Rex unlocked the car and reached into the door pocket for a road map of Derbyshire. He unfolded it and located the A6/A38 ring road with his finger. "Aye, Little Eaton is up that way."

"Trey's parents live at the Old Rectory, a lovely property with stables, according to Ada. His father, who's American, is something big in computer chips. Trey's fifteen-year-old sister attends a private school and his younger brother is at Durham University."

Rex smiled at his wife. "Been sleuthing?"

"Absolutely. I complimented Ada on the catering and gave her a hand packing up. I don't think she realized I was your better half, I just said I knew Penny. We got to talking about Trey, whom I said was a credit to his parents. Ada told me she knew them well from charity events. They're an extremely close family, apparently."

"How did they feel about Cassie?"

"They adored her. They were a bit surprised by the quick engagement, but fully supportive."

"Did Ada say anything else?"

"Only that Trey is very cut up over Cassie and is not eating or sleeping. She's worried about his health. He did look extremely pale."

"Aye, poor lad. It's not surprising."

Trey Atkins appeared to have had everything going for him, until his beautiful fiancée was brutally taken away before they could publicly announce their engagement.

NINETEEN

LATER THAT EVENING, A phone call interrupted Rex and Helen's quiet dinner at home.

"It's Penny," he said after removing the mobile from his pocket and viewing the screen.

"You had better answer it. It must be important for her to be ringing you."

He did so. "Hello, Penny. Before I forget: no joy at the corner shop. I popped in there after the service, but neither the owner nor his son, who helps out, remember a man in a long, black, buttoned coat coming in on Friday. Any news at your end?" he asked hopefully. Presumably, it wasn't a social call.

"Well, yes, actually."

"Wait a second while I put you on speaker. Helen's with me. Go on, Penny."

"Inspector Fiske has taken Christopher Ells in for further questioning." Penny's sophisticated voice reverberated from the phone. "Paul Reddit rang me about it. The inspector and his sergeant paid

Christopher a house call this evening. He was cooperative and let them look around his flat, and it appears they found some incriminating items. Of course, Paul didn't use the word incriminating, because he's undertaken Christopher's defence, but what they discovered was enough for the detectives to arrest him."

"Paul told me he doesn't practise criminal law."

"He'll be doing it as a favour. If Christopher is charged with murder, Paul will no doubt find an experienced barrister to defend him."

"What did the detectives find?"

"He wouldn't say. I thought you could find out more. I can't pretend I'm altogether surprised. I mean, of everyone involved in the play, Christopher Ells was somewhere at the top of my list."

"Because?"

"Well, mostly because he's a bit strange. Dark. I don't know; it's just a feeling. But at the same time, it's a relief. I was going out of my mind with uncertainty. And then today at the memorial service, I kept thinking, Is it her? Is it him?"

"I know what you mean." Rex had been viewing everyone with suspicion as well. "That certainly is an interesting development. Thanks for filling us in, Penny." He ended the call and pensively took up his knife and fork.

He had not expected such a speedy arrest. And to be honest with himself, he felt slightly miffed. When had Fiske decided Christopher Ells was a prime suspect? He had spoken with the inspector only that afternoon, and Fiske had never let on, although he had said something about Ells being the most reticent of the witnesses.

However, that in and of itself did not warrant a home visit. He would call Paul Reddit after dinner and find out what he could.

"Does that mean you're off the case?" Helen asked with a sympathetic expression.

"It rather looks that way." Rex cut into a roast potato. "I'm a little surprised. I mean, Ells' alibi is perhaps not as airtight as some of the others', but ..." he trailed off with a mystified shrug.

The butler had been spotted on the backstage steps taking a snifter of gin, but had anyone really been paying close attention at that point? Rodney Snyder had noticed him, but had been busy on his phone, as had Dennis Caldwell and Andrew Forsythe, and Tony had been working on lessons for his primary schoolers. Could Ells have run up onstage, shot Cassie, and returned to the stairs before anyone realized he had been gone? Just possibly. And what were the items found at his flat?

Rex sighed and said to Helen, "Ah, well, let's see what Mr. Reddit has to say."

At first, the solicitor did not have much to say at all, wishing to respect his client's privacy, but professional courtesy or curiosity as to what the Scottish barrister might make of the potential evidence ultimately prompted him to agree to divulge the information, subject to Rex promising confidentiality on his part.

"You have my absolute discretion," Rex assured him.

"All right then. *Hur-rum.* A packet of thin latex gloves, allegedly stolen from the hospital where Ells works, and identical to one found in the playing fields by Hill Grange Community Centre, was discovered at his flat. But more significant, perhaps," said the solicitor, "is what Inspector Fiske described as a shrine dedicated to Cassie in his bedroom."

"A shrine?" Rex repeated with interest.

"Photos and newspaper clippings of her, pre-dating her death, pasted on the wall, and news stories pertaining to her demise stored in a folder in a desk drawer. Those relating to her roles in local productions go back a year. Some of the photos are amateur close-ups of her taken in a pub."

"Possibly after the dress rehearsal on Wednesday, when they all went to celebrate. Any cartridges matching the murder weapon?" Clearly, the detectives were now treating the shooting as a murder.

"No, nothing like that. However …" The solicitor hesitated at the other end of the line.

"There's something else?" Rex probed.

"*Hur-rum,* yes. It seems our Mr. Ells has a criminal record."

This was what must have led Fiske to make further inquiries. "What sort of criminal record?"

"Assault and battery of an ex-wife," Reddit revealed with a resigned sigh. "Five years ago. He received a suspended sentence."

"A history of violence against women. But no smoking gun," Rex summarized.

"He hasn't been charged yet. They've put him in a cell overnight. Mr. Ells appointed me to represent him, but I'm feeling rather out of my depth. I'll see him through the preliminaries, but if he's remanded in custody, I'll have to find him someone with experience in murder trials."

"Is it your opinion Ells murdered Cassie Chase?"

"Of course not," Reddit answered dutifully. "But Inspector Fiske appears to think otherwise."

After the call, Rex settled back in the living room armchair and mulled over how strong a case the police had against Ells. He was perhaps the only member of the cast and production team whose movements were not fully accounted for. His obsession with Cassie had been going on for a year, long before rehearsals had begun for *Peril at Pinegrove Hall*, as indicated by the newspaper articles in his possession. And yet, when the inspector and sergeant had visited his home, their suspect had let them take a look around, on the surface suggesting he felt he had nothing to hide. That he had latex gloves of the same type found near the community centre was circumstantial at best, as a defence lawyer would argue in court.

Rex returned with his empty tea mug to the kitchen, where Helen was loading towels into the washing machine.

"Does it look bad for the butler?" she asked, glancing up from her task.

"Mr. Reddit swore me to secrecy, so I can't get into specifics, but Ells is a viable suspect. I have little choice but to leave the case to the police. Considering we're heading back to Edinburgh tomorrow, it's probably just as well."

"You won't be happy," Helen predicted as she closed the porthole door of the machine. "Incidentally, Julie rang just now wondering if, in the course of your conversations with Mike Fiske, he may have mentioned her."

Rex shook his head, taking no pleasure in breaking the news. "I think he was quite taken with you, though."

"Well, I'm already taken," his wife said airily. "So, no hope for Julie then?"

"Perhaps she could try the bass guitarist in the band she mentioned. He may have more appealing arms than the drummer."

"Rex, you are too wicked. I know how you feel about Julie, but I've known her since university, and we've been through a lot together. She's like a sister."

"I know, and I like Julie well enough, I do. I just wish sometimes she would act her age."

Helen expelled a sigh. "Well, I can't disagree with you there."

Rex crossed the kitchen and took her in his arms. "Let's forget about Julie's love life and the case for the time being and watch our wedding."

They had seen the DVD only once, with Rex's mother, the night before they had driven to Derby for the long weekend.

"Lovely idea," Helen said, hugging him close and calling him a big softie. She picked the laundry basket off the floor.

"A sherry?" he asked.

"Please."

Rex poured the drinks and took them into the living room, where he set them down on the coffee table and opened his lap top. From his briefcase, he retrieved the two CD-ROMs capturing for posterity their traditional Scottish wedding in the Highlands, replete with swords and bagpipes. The first disc contained the marriage ceremony at Gleneagle Kirk; the second, the lavish reception at his nearby country retreat, an erstwhile hunting lodge located on a secluded loch.

A wedding planner had orchestrated the banquet down to the flower arrangements and tartan napkins, the menu a sumptuous spread of delicacies, including smoked salmon and roast beef, and a giant champagne sorbet in the shape of two swans, garnished with fruit.

His wife joined him on the sofa and they settled down to watch the opening panoramic view of the sun-dappled moors, purple with heather, surrounding the ancient stone church. The guests in elegant hats gathered outside, waiting for the groom and bride to arrive, Rex pulling up with his son Campbell and his colleague Alistair Frazer in one chauffeur-driven limousine, and Helen, ten minutes later, in another, accompanied by her sister Corinne and Julie, matron and maid-of-honour.

Finally, the big moment. Helen, serene in a cream silk gown and a sheer stiff veil crowned with yellow roses. Rex removing the long white glove from her left hand in preparation for slipping on the wedding band. And then catastrophe. A hungover Alistair had misplaced the ring, causing panic at the altar while he searched through the pockets of his gold silk waistcoat and pinstripe trousers. After a few anxious moments, he produced it with a flourish, and Rex realized that his friend had done it in jest and shot him a look promising to get him back later. Helen laughed into her chest and guests in the front pews chuckled. The minister pronounced them man and wife.

The solemn kiss, soft and lingering, had been sublime, Rex filled with such a sense of contentment and completeness that he had taken his hands from Helen's radiant face and pumped his fists in the air, and the church had echoed with cheers.

Just then, his phone went off for the second time that night, yanking him back to the present. The mantelpiece clock softly chimed nine o'clock.

"Who can that be now?" Helen asked, reaching for her sherry on the coffee table.

Rex studied the number on his phone. "I don't know, but at least we didn't miss the best part of the wedding. Rex Graves," he answered.

"It's Tim Holden," burst an urgent voice at the other end. "I'm phoning from the police station on Prime Park Way, Chester Green. Can you come? Ells ratted me out."

TWENTY

REX FOUND ST. MARY'S Wharf Divisional Headquarters looming behind heavy metal gates, the utilitarian brick building with its narrow windows and side tower promoting a sense of foreboding. Special arrangements had been made to gain Rex access to the custody suite, where Inspector Fiske met him at the front desk with a warm handshake and thanked the uniformed sergeant for taking care of his visitor.

"Holden didn't have any family to call, so I let him contact you," Fiske explained.

"To tell the truth, I was even more surprised to learn he was here than I was when I heard Christopher Ells had been brought in. Holden said his friend Ells had implicated him in the murder, but he refused to give me any details over the phone."

"Ells was no doubt trying to deflect suspicion from himself by making Holden look bad. He said Holden had watched snuff films with him and had confessed to fantasizing about killing someone onstage in front of an audience."

Rex checked his surprise. "No accounting for taste," he remarked, ever perturbed by the depths of people's depravity. "If making a snuff film were the motive for Cassie's murder, you'd expect some recording of the event, no?"

"We're looking on Ells' laptop. We didn't find any flash drives, but those little buggers are easy to conceal."

"Did anyone see someone filming the opening night?" Rex recalled that signs in the hall expressly prohibited the use of mobile phones during a performance.

The inspector shook his head. "None of the spectators noticed anything."

"In any case, it's impossible Holden shot Cassie if Ada Case and Susan Richardson returned with him backstage after visiting the lavatories."

"The two women do corroborate Holden's alibi," Fiske confirmed. "But before we release him, see if you can get anything out of him. It seems he was quite chummy with Ells. It should be illegal to watch snuff material, but how to monitor it all?" Fiske rubbed the bags under his bleary eyes. "Forgive the rant, Rex. I need some coffee. Fancy some?"

Rex declined, having no palate for police station coffee, which seemed to impregnate the walls with its stale aroma. After grabbing one for himself, the inspector led him upstairs and down a corridor with a succession of numerically lettered doors on either side. Detective Sergeant Antonescu stood outside Interview Room Two, arms crossed against his chest, eyes peering beneath his menacing eyebrows. He gave a brief if not very encouraging nod as he stepped aside to permit Rex to enter the room.

Timothy Holden sat at a bare table in front of a white paper cup, facing an observation window in the wall. He had changed out of the shirt and tie he had worn at the memorial service and into a long-sleeved grey sweatshirt mottled with bleach stains. His jutting chin exhibited late-night shadow, his dazed face sickly pale beneath the flickering fluorescent strip lighting that emitted a continuous electric hum. As Rex sat down in one of the two extra chairs, he noted dark shadows circling Holden's eyes, enlarged behind his glasses.

"Thanks for coming," Holden said with a pitiful sigh of relief.

"How can I help?"

"Like I said on the phone, I didn't do nothing, but I don't want to talk to the detectives. They'll hammer me for hours until I can't think straight. On the other hand, if I insist on a lawyer, it might make me look guilty. And it's a lottery with public defenders, innit, with no more chance of a win than with a million-pound scratch-off. So, what d'you advise?"

Rex could be sure the two detectives were listening in on the other side of the blind window. "I cannot advise you. For one thing, I only practise Scottish law."

"Fat lot of use that is."

"Rest assured, if the guilty party is found, you have nothing to worry about."

"Well, hurry it up, yeh? I'm innocent! How much longer do I have to sit in here? I'm freezing my nuts off."

Rex perceived it wasn't only the frigid temperature that made the room cold. Everything, from the minimalist furnishings to the dingy walls displaying crime prevention posters, was designed to optimize discomfort and demoralize suspects into submission. He removed his jacket and told Holden to put it around his shoulders, which he did with a touching expression of gratitude.

"Tell me about the snuff films you watched with Ells. That seems to be the main reason you're here."

"It was just a bit of escapism."

Rex wondered what Holden's life was like that he felt the need to resort to snuff films to escape. He tried to imagine him working at the sandwich shop and living alone, probably with no girlfriend in the picture. He was not an attractive proposition for women with his protruding jaw and only the bottom row of teeth visible, ragged and grey. More than likely, Penny's play had been a high point in his monotonous existence.

"There's no real harm in it," Holden went on, defending his viewing choice. "There's worse on the Internet with ISIS beheading people and burning them alive in cages."

"Ells said you wanted to kill someone onstage."

"That's a lie! Or if I said anything like that, it was under the influence of one too many. It was just beer talk."

"So, Cassie Chase's death in front of a live audience was purely coincidental?"

"It wasn't me! Anyway, her death was offstage. No one saw nothing. Except the killer, of course, who might've videoed it."

"Unlikely they had time."

"They could've worn a camera and rolled the video while in motion." Holden planted his elbows on the table, closed his eyes, and shook his head wearily. "Even if I wanted to kill someone, it would never be Cassie."

Rex feared Holden might clam up if he persisted with the current line of questioning. "I, personally, am more interested in why Penny said she had seen you at the community centre on Friday, almost an hour prior to your stated time of arrival of five forty."

Holden looked up in surprise. "Why would she say that?"

"You tell me."

"Same reason as Chris," the detainee replied glumly. "To put the blame somewhere else, or maybe she's covering for someone. Penny Spencer has a wild imagination. She wrote the play, after all. And she doesn't like me. She never wanted me in the play even though I looked enough the part and the Father Brown costume fit. Rodney told me. He said Mr. Reddit had asked him to coach me on my lines so I could, in his words, deliver an acceptable Essex accent. I had less than two weeks to prepare because the first Father Brown was leaving before the play opened. I'd have asked Mr. Reddit to represent me, but Ells got to him first."

"Did you meet the person who had the part before you? Penny mentioned he left the play to pursue an acting career in the States."

Holden shook his head. "I heard, though, he'd done some TV ads and managed to score a few small parts in films and in a kid's serial playing a track star." He opened his palms on the table in a helpless gesture of entreaty, revealing stubby fingers on his wide hands. "Can you help me, Mr. Graves? It's like everyone's out to get me."

"Sit tight, Mr. Holden, and I'll see what I can do."

"I don't have much choice other than to sit tight, do I?"

Rex got up and recovered his jacket with a word of apology, giving Holden a reassuring pat on the shoulder. Inspector Fiske met him on the other side of the door.

"Playing the victim card, I see," the inspector said with a wry smirk.

"If you're going to release him, I could offer to take him home."

"I'd like to take another crack at him. Maybe he'll change his mind about talking to us now that you've softened him up. Ells is the reason he's here. Perhaps now he'll return the favour and snitch on his friend."

"I wish you luck," Rex said with a small smile of his own. He paused as he turned away. "Could you at least fetch the poor man a blanket or turn up the thermostat?"

"How about a hot water bottle and a mug of Ovaltine while we're at it," jibed Antonescu, shutting the door of the next room and joining them.

"Watch it, son," Fiske told his sergeant. "I hear Mr. Graves is a formidable prosecutor."

"It may be a matter of catching more flies with honey than vinegar," Rex responded mildly to Antonescu's comments.

With a brief nod to the inspector, he made his way back along the interminable corridor, down the stairs to the main entrance, and into the car park, glad when he had left the police complex and the slow late-night lorries far behind him on the parkway.

By the time he returned to Barley Close, Helen was already in bed, wearing a lacy nightdress and sitting up against the pillows in the soft light cast by the reading lamp. She slipped the pattern-framed glasses off her nose and bookmarked the page of her novel.

"Couldn't sleep?" he asked.

"I didn't even try. Not sure I could, alone in the house. How did you get on? You have that cat-and-canary look about you. Don't deny it!"

Rex removed his jacket and sat down on her side of the bed. "I do have a theory, but it is only a theory at this point. I really need to talk to Penny again."

Helen furrowed her brow. "It's too late to ring her."

"I'll try her first thing in the morning. If I'm on the right track, it may mean delaying our return to Edinburgh by a day or two."

"Well, I'm temporarily unemployed, and you have the rest of the week off, so it's not really a problem, except that your mother is expecting us for dinner."

"I'll call her as soon as I have a better idea of where I am in the case. She's used to my erratic schedule."

"But what about Julie? She's supposed to be moving in tomorrow afternoon. I don't think she could stand another night at her mum's."

Rex took his wife's hand and kissed her palm. "She can still move in tomorrow. It'll be company for you while I'm off hopefully solving the case."

He gave her fingers a quick squeeze and rose from the bed to undress.

"But you don't think it's the butler or Father Brown?"

Rex turned towards Helen as he continued to unbutton his shirt, and merely smiled. She retaliated by throwing a pillow at him.

"You are insufferable," she said, snuggling down into the bed. "But I correctly guessed the fictitious murderer, don't forget."

"You did. Robin Busket, the interloper at Pinegrove Hall. But I don't think Cassie's killer is going to so conveniently trip up and spill the beans, more's the pity."

At that moment, a sudden spring rain began pattering against the panes. Rex looked out behind the curtains at the windows in the houses on the opposite side of the street, for the most part clothed in darkness, only a few blurry yellow squares attesting to wakeful residents or nightmare-prone children.

He would not have to put on the lawn sprinklers, after all, he reflected as he watched droplets of water wiggle down the glass. He reclosed the red crêpe curtains and finished getting ready for bed. Nothing at that moment was more appealing than holding Helen in his arms and being lulled to sleep by the rain.

TWENTY-ONE

REX PHONED PENNY AT half past eight the next morning, asking if she might be free for a brief chat that day. He could come to the school if necessary.

"My first class isn't until one," she said. "I'm off to a doctor's appointment now, but we could meet back at my house, say at eleven?"

He told her that would be perfect and rang off, feeling energized with a new sense of purpose. From across the kitchen table, Helen glanced up from her coffee cup. "Doesn't look like we'll be setting off for Edinburgh today, am I right?"

"We might still make it if my hunch falls through, but I'd better tell Mother not to expect us for dinner, rather than have to cancel this afternoon. What remains to be done here?"

"Not much. I'll run to the shops if we're staying, and I can lend Julie a hand moving in. It shouldn't take long. She only has a few bits and bats of furniture." Julie had lived with a succession of boyfriends and had never had a place to call her own.

Rex set out his notes on the table. Nothing concrete existed so far to support his hunch, and he was anxious to meet with Penny and see if he was on the right track. An hour later, he took off in the car, arriving early at Penny's address, where a white Volvo was parked in the driveway.

The French teacher opened the front door before he could ring. "I just got back. Come on in," she said, removing her pantsuit jacket and hanging it on a peg along with her handbag. "I'll make some coffee."

"How did it go at the doctor's?" he asked.

"Okay, I think; fingers crossed. It was my annual checkup. I won't get the results till next week."

She invited him into a compact, ultramodern kitchen with a breakfast bar and stools, and he sat down on one while she proceeded to tip two helpings of ground coffee into a percolator on the counter. A plush grey cat stalked into the kitchen, raised its nose at Rex, and continued towards Penny, weaving around her ankles as she reached for two mugs in an overhead cabinet.

"It's not time for your lunch, Doucie," she cooed, lifting the cat up in her arms and stroking its head. A droning purr erupted, competing with the burble of the coffee machine. "You're not allergic to cats, are you?" she asked Rex.

"Not at all."

"She usually runs away when men come to the house. She must like you."

"Cats are such discerning creatures," he said with a smile.

She deposited the pet on the floor and returned to preparing the coffee. "Sugar?"

"Aye, but I shouldn't. What blend of coffee do you use?" he asked. "It smells delicious."

"A premium French roast. I got spoilt in Paris. I hope you like yours strong."

"I do."

The mug she placed in front of him featured Théophile Steinlen's 1896 black cat poster advertising *Le Chat Noir* cabaret.

"I feel transported to France," he said, helping himself to the matching jug of milk Penny had set on the breakfast bar beside the sugar bowl.

"I admit to feeling a bit nostalgic, but I'm going back this summer, possibly with Tony. He studied art for a year in Paris when he was a student." She parked herself on the stool next to Rex. "Were you able to talk to Paul Reddit? Is that why you wanted to speak with me?"

"I spoke to him last night by phone, and later went to see Timothy Holden at the police station. He was taken in for questioning as well as Christopher Ells." Rex filled Penny in on as much information as he felt able to tell her. "It was during my talk with Holden that I became all but certain there must be another major player in the case."

"Who?" Penny asked in surprise.

Rex held up his hand, forestalling her question. "Bear with me just a minute. At the beginning, there were many potential suspects, but only a narrow window of opportunity. Agreed?"

Penny nodded.

"By cross-referencing alibis, I was able to whittle down the number of suspects to practically zero. Of course, it's always possible someone mistakenly thought they saw someone, or is confused about the time they saw them, or else people are providing false alibis."

Penny stared at her coffee with a puzzled frown. "You really think more than one person could be involved?" She swivelled round on her bar stool and met his gaze full on. "An accomplice?"

"First I need to know more about the actor who was originally in *Peril at Pinegrove Hall*."

"You mean Darrell, who had Father Brown's part before Tim. Yes, but he's in LA. He emailed me a photo of himself, standing in front of the Hollywood Hills."

"When was this?"

"Friday morning. He was wishing me luck for opening night."

"What was he like to work with?"

"Amenable, talented. He got into his role very quickly. I was disappointed when he had to abandon it. It wasn't a big part, but he made it his own." Penny cupped the mug in her lap. "Timothy did his best but he was a poor substitute."

"Why, if Darrell was a talented actor, did he not get a bigger role in your play?"

"Actually, we did consider him for Henry Chalmers. He had the looks and was suave enough, but Trey was taller and had more natural polish, and he sounded more like I imagine Henry Chalmers would speak."

"You mean posh?"

"But without sounding stilted or affected. We had Darrell read Henry Chalmers' lines, and he did a good job, but for Trey it was more his natural speaking voice. Thank goodness Darrell wasn't the leading man. Leaving us in the lurch with that role to fill would have been a catastrophe."

The play had turned out to be a catastrophe nonetheless, Rex noted privately. "Do you have a photo of him?"

"Yes." Penny got up and left the kitchen, returning shortly with her phone and a bright green folder. "This is the photo from Hollywood." She handed Rex her smartphone.

A young man with brownish-blond hair and wearing a black tee-shirt that showed off gym-honed arms and chest muscles smiled with confidence into the camera, the undulating letters of the Hollywood Sign gleaming white behind him in the frame.

"It's a bit dark, so I brought you this headshot of him from my file," Penny said, opening her folder.

Rex returned her phone and took the black-and-white print of *Darrell Brewster: Age 26, 5'8"*, as stated at the bottom of the sheet. "He looks a bit like a young Viggo Mortensen."

"Or a young Liam Neeson."

"My wife likes him."

"All women like him," Penny said, resuming her seat and taking up her coffee mug.

"I would have thought Darrell too good-looking and athletic for Father Brown. The clergyman in the story I read was more nondescript—and older, as I recall, but it was a long time ago."

"Darrell added some padding and wore glasses and what have you. I admit Timothy, apart from his jaw, was closer to the character in appearance, but appearances can be disguised. Anyway, it didn't matter in the end, did it? It all came to nothing. Well, worse than nothing. I wish I had never written the silly play."

"Don't say that. If it were someone's intent to murder Cassie Chase, they would have done so regardless."

"Perhaps." With a deep sigh, Penny got up from the breakfast bar. "I had to fast for my appointment this morning, so I'm going to make myself a sandwich. Can I tempt you?"

"Thanks, but I promised Helen I'd be back for lunch. Can I keep this?" Rex asked, holding up the headshot.

"By all means, but I don't see why you're interested in Darrell. He wasn't around at the time of the shooting. And there's no motive that I can see." Penny opened the refrigerator and pulled out various items.

"How did he get on with Trey? No animosity there because he lost the role of Henry Chalmers to him?"

"As far as I could see it was all fine. Everyone was sorry to see him go."

"Including Cassie?"

"I think so, although I didn't see them together much, outside of interacting in the play. He was on friendlier terms with Susan, and would josh around with Bill, Ben, and Bobbi." Penny glanced over her shoulder at Rex from the sink, where she was rinsing lettuce in a mesh colander. "You think Inspector Fiske has got it all wrong?" She smiled. "Or are you just hoping?"

"I suppose a bit of both," Rex replied truthfully. "But ultimately, I just want the right person arrested. One final thing, Penny. Do you have an address for Cassie's aunt?"

"No, but I have Joanna's, Cassie's mother. They both live on Rosslyn Grove. One sec." She dried her hands on a tea towel and picked up her phone on the breakfast bar, thumbing away for a minute. "I've texted you the address."

Rex thanked her and got up from his stool, taking the headshot of Darrell with him. "I'll keep you informed."

"Please. When are you returning to Edinburgh?"

"Tomorrow, possibly. It all depends."

Penny saw him to the front door, midway scooping up the grey cat trotting after her. Rex waved from the driveway and clambered into the Renault, processing the new information as he drove back to Barley Close. The photos of Darrell Brewster comported more with a TV-track star, such as Holden had mentioned, than with Father Brown. Before his visit to the police station, Rex had assumed Holden's predecessor to be more in the mould of a Timothy Holden; which just went to show it was never safe to assume, he chided himself.

However, Penny had said Darrell and Cassie had not been close, and the young actor seemed more interested in Susan Richardson, whom Dennis Caldwell had confided had had a crush on Trey in a previous production. Perhaps Darrell's attentions were a soothing balm to Susan after Trey's rejection of her. Rex thought about this a bit more and decided it was probably just a bit of harmless flirtation, Susan being a married woman with three teenage children and simply enjoying a boost to her confidence.

None of this gave Darrell a motive to shoot Cassie, even if he was not in Tinsel Town hoping to make a name for himself. Aiming for bigger and brighter things, as Paul Reddit had said in his office, or words to that effect.

A dead end? Rex pulled up in front of Helen's house and sat staring at the beige pebble-dash wall, thinking at the back of his mind that when they came to sell the house, they would do well to paint it over in white to freshen up the façade. That Inspector Fiske possibly had the better of him in the case was his overriding and immediate preoccupation. Christopher Ells was looking like a more logical suspect, after all. And yet, and yet ... Rex argued with himself. Something didn't quite add up to his complete satisfaction.

TWENTY-TWO

"How do you propose to proceed?" Helen asked Rex.

They had just finished lunch in the beer garden of a local pub and were lingering in the sunshine amid other couples and small groups of people in business attire.

"I'd like to speak to someone who knew Cassie best, like her aunt. Penny gave me Cassie's mother's address, though I'd rather not impose on the mother in her time of grief."

"No, it's too soon, and I'm sure she's been questioned enough by the police. Cassie's room must have been combed through for evidence."

"It has. Mike said nothing was found to indicate suicide or who might have shot her. Unfortunately, she misplaced her mobile the day before her death, and so a lot of phone history was lost with it."

"Surely the police can get hold of her phone records from the phone company," Helen said, pulling out a compact and a gold capsule of lipstick from her handbag.

"Phone numbers can be retrieved, certainly, and the contents of text messages, but it can take a while to get hold of them. They have Trey's. Nothing there to indicate anything was other than a bed of roses between them. She was saving herself for marriage, according to Mike. No wonder Trey proposed so quickly."

"Rex, really," Helen said, returning her compact and lipstick to her bag, her mouth pearly pink again. "Ready?"

In unison, they got up from their table and crossed the trodden grass to the gate leading into a walled-in car park. Rex dropped Helen off at the house and made his way to the address once inhabited by Cassie Chase, which he found in an established residential street in a quiet leafy suburb south of Barley Close.

As he surveyed the opposing rows of well-maintained homes and mature trees, his heart plummeted when he saw the L-shaped bungalow with a concrete ramp leading up to the widened frosted glass door. A large bow window to the left looked out to the street; another, on the shorter projection of wall, faced into the garden, where spring flowers bordered the front of the enviably green lawn.

Parked by the kerb, he turned off the ignition. He had no intention of going up to the door and disturbing Cassie's mother; he just wanted to get an idea of where her daughter had lived, so he might form a fuller picture of the victim.

He had the aunt's surname in his notes from when Ron Wade had introduced her at the memorial service, and entered "Belinda Stokes" and the street name into the search engine on his phone. Before he could read the first entry, a double tap on the car window startled him. Whipping his head around, he found himself staring into a pair of gentian blue eyes. Belinda's face, lowered to his level, displayed a hesitant smile.

He pressed open the window. "You're just the person I wanted to see," he said, handing over his card from his wallet.

"I recognized you from the service. A QC from Scotland," she read with the aid of a pair of gold-rimmed spectacles hung on a chain around her neck. "I feel honoured." She smiled at him fully at that point and straightened up, stepping back from the car.

Rex got out and closed the door. "I'm helping the police with their inquiries, but not in the sense it's usually understood."

"I gathered as much. I'm staying at my sister's for now. I was just taking a break in the garden while she napped. We can talk there. I heard the car engine and came to see who it might be, ready to chase away any reporter before they could ring the bell and wake her."

He followed Belinda up the short driveway and through a gate in a white trellis fence enclosing a patio, which accommodated four white wrought-iron chairs arranged around a table of the same ornate design. Hybrid tea roses with blush and yellow petals, rather like the ones he had got Helen, fluttered gently in a flowerbed running along the brick wall of the house. A bee buzzed lazily over the blossoms in the warm breeze.

"Sit yourself down while I fetch some lemonade," Belinda offered, proceeding towards the back of the bungalow.

Rex took a seat. A sketch pad and a B pencil with a thick soft point lay on the table. He saw that the rose bed was the subject of Belinda's drawing. Through the white trelliswork, the occasional car and pedestrian passed by in the early afternoon sunshine.

"You're an artist?" he asked when Belinda returned with two tall glasses and a jug rattling with ice on a tray.

"It's mostly just a hobby, though I do get a bit of commissioned work." She sat down and poured the lemonade. "I find it therapeutic to concentrate on nature during times of great sadness and stress." She contemplated the roses, the source of her inspiration for her latest sketch. "I wish I'd pursued art in school, but the guidance counsellor persuaded me to take shorthand, arguing it was more vocational. I doubt people have used shorthand since the advent of Dictaphones. Still, it got me a decent job in an office after I left school."

She flipped back the stiff pages of her pad. "I do pet portraits mainly. This is Peekaboo, Cassie's dog." She showed Rex drawings of a shaggy-haired Pekinese with short legs and a black snout. "Called Boo for short. She hasn't left Cassie's bed other than to stand by the front door at specific times waiting for her to come home. It's heartbreaking. She knows something's amiss."

Belinda's face saddened, but lost none of its serenity. Her smooth skin radiated a heathy glow, which he perceived to be natural. She did not appear to be wearing makeup other than a pale coat of lipstick and possibly a hint of mascara around her eyes. An assortment of silver and turquoise stone jewellery adorned her fingers, ear lobes, and neck above the embroidered, white peasant blouse. A brown dirndl skirt and beaded sandals completed her bohemian style of dress.

Rex took a drink of his lemonade. "Ah, just what I needed."

"Fresh-squeezed and organic," she said, raising her glass to her lips. She paused. "To Cassie," she toasted. "And may we get the brute who did this to you, my dearest darling."

"You don't think she took her own life, then?" Rex asked cautiously.

Belinda shook her silvery mass of hair. "Heavens, no. It would have been a shamefully dramatic and inconsiderate thing to do, and our Cassie wasn't like that. She had a zeal for life and was devoted to her mother. Joanna sometimes has difficulty even opening her pill bottles and swallowing. Cassie would never leave her voluntarily. In any case, if she had truly wanted to end her life, it would not have been with a gun. She was vehemently anti-guns."

"I too am convinced she didn't take her own life, but it seems someone wanted to make it appear so."

"Have you come to tell me you know who?"

Rex placed his empty glass on the table. "I was hoping you might be able to help me with that. Any ideas?"

"Not positively. I don't know the other actors in the play apart from Trey, except to say hello. Is Penny not able to help you?"

"She had more of a working relationship with them. She didn't even know for certain that Trey and Cassie were going steady."

"No, well, there was a good reason why they tried to keep that a secret."

Rex fixed his gaze on her. "Someone else would have been jealous?" he ventured.

Belinda nodded. "Cassie was being stalked. It doesn't matter by who, since he left before this awful thing happened, otherwise I'd be looking at him for her murder. It's not unusual, men killing their ex-girlfriends because they don't want anyone else to have them. That's not love; it's selfish, controlling behaviour."

Rex wondered if Belinda spoke from direct experience. He had noticed she did not wear a wedding band. "Was this person Darrell Brewster?"

Belinda met his gaze. "So, you know about him."

"I know he was originally in the play, not that he stalked your niece. In fact, no one I've spoken to mentioned he had feelings for Cassie." But now, Rex had the connection he sought.

"They may not have been aware. Cassie had broken off with him long before *Peril at Pinegrove Hall*, but he didn't give up."

"Why did she split up with him? Was it because of Trey?"

Belinda distractedly smoothed down a bent corner of her sketch pad with her slim fingers. "No, that came after. Everything was wonderful at first. Darrell was very attentive and always thinking up fun things for them to do that didn't cost money. He was a bit-part actor, mainly playing petty criminals on TV and appearing in a few nonspeaking parts in films, and had to live with his mother out of financial necessity. He was often here playing cards and board games with Cassie and Joanna, who's becoming increasingly housebound. He was very good with her; Joanna, I mean. Cassie had a full plate, what with helping take care of her mum, work, and theatre; and the moment she started pulling away, he began to get possessive. Now, Cassie wasn't about to let anyone dictate to her what to do. Besides, she wanted stability. She had her mother to consider."

Belinda smiled, adding, "And the height thing bothered her. One day she told me, 'Auntie, if I marry Darrell, I won't be able to wear heels on my wedding day.' Of course, Darrell's prospects might change in Los Angeles. Perhaps it was his aim to impress her and then come back and sweep her off her feet. I received a long text from him on Sunday, as a matter of fact. Obviously, he's stunned. His mother had given him the devastating news."

"Was she at the memorial service?" Rex asked.

"I don't know. I had to take my sister home." Belinda took a quick sip of lemonade. "Perhaps I shouldn't have said that about Darrell being capable of killing my niece. It's not really fair."

"Did he ever display violence towards her?"

"Nothing provable. One of her tyres punctured by a roof nail. Some ripped clothing in her room, which could have been Boo with her little claws. A gold chain with a heart pendant from Trey that went missing, but which she thought might have come apart at work when she was removing her apron. Mostly just a barrage of calls and text messages, and small gifts and flowers. He left a red rose and a note on the doorstep before he took off for the States."

"What did she do with the note?"

"What she always did. Crumpled it up and threw it away. She didn't want Trey finding it. And Boo got out of the garden a month ago, through this gate." Belinda glanced towards the trellis fence. "However, we're careful about keeping it shut. We knew what Boo meant to Cassie. She went out of her mind when we couldn't find her. Fortunately, late the next day a neighbour spotted Boo in the garden of a derelict house almost a mile away."

"That's a long walk for a little dog."

"If she walked," Belinda said meaningfully. "Boo's collar with her name and phone number was missing too, but she was unharmed; just hungry and very frightened."

"Did you like Darrell before you suspected him of doing these things?"

"Yes, but I did tell Cassie she was short-changing herself. And then Trey came along. They met doing *The Lady of Shalott*. She had the title role and he played Sir Lancelot."

"So I heard," Rex said. Perhaps Cassie's fate was sealed the moment she became enamoured of Trey, just as the Lady of Shalott's curse had been fulfilled the day she set eyes on the dashing Lancelot.

"And then they were in this latest play together. They were a perfect match." With a faraway look in her eyes, Belinda gazed up at the azure sky beyond the tiled roof. "Why can't she be sharing this idyllic day with us? I couldn't have children of my own," she confided suddenly. "My niece was such a blessing. I keep thinking how unfair it all is."

Rex reached out and patted her hand.

"Please catch the person who did this. It won't bring her back, but it may help make more sense of what happened."

Rex promised he would do his utmost.

TWENTY-THREE

BELINDA HAD TOLD REX where Darrell Brewster lived with his mother in Littleover, a village a few miles southwest of Derby city centre, and he drove straight there, only to find no one home.

Mrs. Doreen Brewster was a widow, Belinda had informed him, and was employed as a clerk for the post office. She must still be at work, he realized, but rang the bell again for good measure, hearing the tinny chime behind the door of the stark brick bungalow. Still no human sound from inside the house. Rex decided to drive out to the Old Rectory, unannounced, to find Trey. The police probably still had Trey's phone and Rex felt he would get more out of the young man if they could talk in person, away from Ada and the others, and on his own turf.

Brick row houses, old churches, and seedy shops passed by his open car windows as he drove into downtown Derby among a stream of rumbling buses and honking cars and taxis. The air in the Renault was close and fume-ridden. He temporarily released his seat belt and wrestled out of his jacket. The AC was in dire need of a tune-up, yet another item on his to-do list.

Finally, he left the city behind, proceeding north on Alfreton Road into the countryside. A cleansing breeze blew in through the windows as he sped along to the sound of the radio tuned into a classic rock station. His mood lightened and his thoughts flew to his forthcoming honeymoon and recent wedding. So engrossed was he in memories of the ceremony that he drove past the sign for the Old Rectory and had to execute a three-point turn in the wooded lane.

He headed back to the open ornamental gates and followed a gravel driveway flanked by lawns and rhododendron bushes to a square, mid-Georgian house, the mellowed red brick, stone quoins, and parapet draped in ivy. His tyres crunched to a stop beside Trey's blue BMW, and he got out and stood for a moment surveying the residence. Though not as grand as many country homes he had seen in Derbyshire, the Old Rectory had clearly belonged to a well-to-do parson, and he could readily visualize carriages pulling up to the gabled portico entrance that was supported on a pair of white pillars.

He climbed the short flight of steps to the smart black door surmounted by a fanlight with intricate radial tracery, and pressed the brass bell. No one answered, but it was a sizeable house, and he surmised Trey could be in the deepest recesses of it. He waited several minutes before trying again. Just then, he heard the clopping of horse hooves coming from beyond the residence and headed in that direction.

In a cobblestone courtyard stood two pure-bred stallions with sleek brown coats and flowing ivory tails, waiting docilely while their riders dismounted. One of the individuals was a teenage girl in jodhpurs and riding boots, a blonde ponytail cascading down the back of her polo-neck jersey from beneath her black velvet hat. Her companion, similarly dressed, he recognized as Mr. Reddit's niece. Both watched warily as he approached. A white-and-tan Collie emerged from the group and sat down, drooling and panting, at his feet. Rex guessed it had gone out with the riders.

"Hello, Miss Shaw. And you must be Trey's sister," he said, stopping a safe distance from the horses, harbouring a childhood distrust of the equine breed and not wishing to startle them. They eyed him sideways, their tails swishing at the flies that beset them. "I'm Rex Graves, an acquaintance of your brother. I tried ringing the doorbell. Is he around?"

"I'm not sure. We just got back from a trek." The girl was tall and fine-featured like Trey, with the same pale, lightly freckled skin. "Is his BMW parked out front?"

"It is."

"Then he can't be far." She handed her reins and riding crop to Bobbi. "Could you see to Brett for me? Thanks."

Bobbi led the two horses towards the stables on the far side of the courtyard while the girl took Rex to a back door of the house, which opened outwards before they could reach it.

"Mr. Graves here has been looking for you," she told her brother in an annoyed tone of voice.

"Sorry," he said to Rex. "I looked out the window and didn't recognize the car."

"It could have been for me," his sister reproached him.

"It could equally well have been the press. Mr. Graves, please come in—and excuse the mess. Abby, you go and help Bobbi."

Trey retreated into a clay-tiled mud room, which housed a rectangular stone sink and an old wooden table covered with trowels, packets of seeds, a stack of flower pots, and a pair of women's gardening gloves. An assortment of anoraks and fleece jackets hung from an iron coat rack. Wellington boots, galoshes, fishing tackle, and a Badminton net lay in a mildewy heap below the outdoor garments. Clearly, the Atkins family embraced the country life with open arms.

Rex followed the young man into a spacious flagstone kitchen featuring an eight-ring gas burner range in stainless steel, above which a collection of pans dangled in order of size beneath the giant hood.

"I was surprised to see Bobbi Shaw here," Rex said, planting himself in the middle of the floor. "Although, come to mention it, her uncle did tell me she liked horses."

"She helps out with ours, mucking out and exercising them when my parents are away. I'm getting tea for everyone. Will you join us?"

"Gladly. When is your mother due home?"

"Tonight, thankfully." Trey filled a kettle at the farmhouse sink. "Abby is being a right little brat, as you can see."

"She's at that age, I suppose."

"No consideration for anyone but herself."

While Trey busied himself with the tea, Rex walked over to a large bay window and stood for a moment contemplating the walled vegetable garden, where spring cabbage and radishes sprouted in the tilled earth, and raspberry canes grew in orderly rows. It was hard not to make comparisons between this comfortable property and the modest bungalow where Mrs. Brewster lived with her son.

He leaned back against the window sill. "You must think I keep turning up like a bad penny, but I spoke to Cassie's aunt this afternoon and she was able to confirm a suspicion I had regarding a certain Darrell Brewster, and I hoped you could enlighten me further."

Trey, a glazed pottery teapot in one hand and two matching mugs in the other, halted in his tracks on the way to the knotted pine table by a second window. "Did she tell you he'd been stalking Cassie?"

"Aye. It's relevant information, don't you think?"

Trey continued to the table and set down the items. "If he were still in England," he agreed, "but he's not." He looked directly at Rex, his chiselled face evenly lit by the natural lighting from the window. "Although it did cross my mind that the call you received might have been him calling from the States. That would be just like him, to impersonate me."

"The call came from a petrol station not far from here, on Sunday. And the caller did sound a bit like you."

"You're saying he's here? In Derby?" The young man's Adam's apple moved as he swallowed. "He can't be."

"I don't know for certain. Penny showed me a photo she received from him on Friday morning, taken of him in Hollywood with the iconic sign in the background. But the picture might have been photoshopped. When was the last time you saw him?"

"Wednesday, at the dress rehearsal. He was filming it."

"Excuse me?" Rex asked in surprise. "Are you sure?"

"Yes. He was standing towards the back of the hall with a tripod-mounted camcorder."

That at least made sense since the play had been recorded in a wide shot. Rex tried to picture Darrell videoing the rehearsal as it unfolded onstage; the would-be murderer behind the lens, perhaps.

Trey stared out of the window, as though not really seeing the view. "It was his parting gift, he said. And a memento for him to remember us all by. And now you're saying he never left?" He turned around to face Rex.

"I didn't know he was still around on Wednesday," Rex mused aloud, his mind busy with time sequences.

"He hadn't been by in a while, and he didn't come to the pub with us afterwards. He said he had to pack for his flight in the morning."

"I thought Ben had shot the dress rehearsal, since he was the one who gave Penny the DVD."

"Ben had to work backstage with Bill. There's a lot goes on behind the scenes."

"Apparently," Rex said with irony, recalling the events of opening night.

Trey flopped into the chair at the head of the table. "It was him. Darrell. He shot Cassie," he said in a stunned voice.

"First we need to prove he was still in Derby on Friday." Rex took a seat on the cushioned pine bench running the length of the table beneath the window. "Tell me exactly what happened between him and Cassie."

Trey straightened in the chair. "She'd dumped him, but he was not ready to give up. Darrell Brewster has a massive chip on his shoulder. He acted like everything was cool, but I always felt it was just that—an act. There was an incident early on in our relationship where a figure dressed from head to foot in black jumped onto the bonnet of my car as we were leaving a restaurant. I swerved, almost hitting a wall. As it was, he left a dent in the bodywork, which I had to get fixed. Cassie was terrified. At the time, I thought it was a mugger and I called the police."

"Was he arrested?"

"No, he ran off, and although Cassie said she knew who it was, we couldn't prove it. That's when it all came out about the stalking. It was apparent he was trying to scare me off, but she said she wasn't going to let him get between us and she assured me she could deal with it. I suggested she apply for a restraining order, but she said it wouldn't be fair to him because then he'd essentially be banned from local theatre, as it might look like he was harassing her."

"Was it not a wee bit awkward with the three of you in the same play?" Rex enquired. Darrell must have felt the sting of losing the role of Henry Chalmers to Trey, her new boyfriend. On the other hand, taking a lesser part had kept him close to Cassie, and perhaps he had hoped to win her back.

"We played down our relationship so as not to provoke him, even though it had been over between them for months. But then he seemed to take an interest in Susan, which was a bit odd, considering the age difference and the fact she's married, but, whatever. It was a relief to us both."

"Especially as Susan had been sweet on you?"

A blush spread over Trey's well-defined cheek bones. "I never encouraged her. And, anyway, she got over it. It's not uncommon to take a fancy to someone you're supposed to have an emotional connection with in a play, especially since you're working so closely together. That's why so many big-name actors end up in relationships with their co-stars."

"Which often fail," Rex remarked, "no doubt because the illusion doesn't live up to reality. Another thing: could Darrell have stolen Cassie's mobile?" Perhaps her stalker had left texts on it that he would have preferred the police not find in the event of her death.

Trey's gaze drifted across the room to the white-washed wall. "It went missing Thursday night," he said wonderingly. "Cassie rang me at around eight and said she was going to watch TV with her mum. When I phoned her the next morning, her mobile went straight to voicemail. She finally rang me on Joanna's phone to say she had misplaced hers, although she was sure she had left it in her room after we had spoken the night before."

"Her aunt told me she thought Darrell had been in her room before and had ripped up some of her clothes. Could she have left her bedroom window open?"

"It's possible. They don't have air conditioning in the house, and she made do with a floor fan." Trey's chin dropped to his chest. "She never mentioned about the clothes. I suppose she didn't want me going after him. There's probably loads more she didn't tell me. I can't tell you how happy I was when I found out he was going to LA and could be gone for months." He wrung his hands in his lap, a pained expression on his face. "It's hard to admit I wasn't able to protect her. If it was him, I'll never be able to forgive myself."

At that point in the conversation, Trey's sister burst into the kitchen from the utility room, accompanied by Bobbi, both in their socks and bringing in with them a whiff of the stables.

"Where's tea?" Abby scolded. "Oh, my God, I have to do everything myself."

She disappeared into the pantry while Bobbi stood by gawkily, fluffing up her short auburn hair which had been flattened by the riding hat.

"Bobbi," Rex said, breaking the strained silence. "We were discussing Darrell Brewster. How well did you know him?"

Her eyes slid first to Trey, who remained unresponsive at the table. "Pretty well, I suppose," she said in her husky voice. "He had the role of Father Brown originally but had to relinquish it when he got the chance to be in a hospital drama on a major American cable network. He wasn't at the community centre much these past weeks, but he came by last Wednesday to say goodbye to everyone. We were all sorry to see him go."

Trey lightly raised his eyebrows, but said nothing. Abby breezed back to the table and plonked down a round tin containing walnut cake and a cutting board holding a loaf of bread. She then strode to a refrigerator disguised behind a distressed wood door panel and extracted a butter dish and a pot of homemade jam covered with a brown paper lid, which she likewise deposited on the table, directing an exasperated look at her brother.

"Mr. Graves, shall I get you a plate?" she asked politely, suddenly remembering her manners.

"Thank you, but I should probably get going. I have another stop to make."

Trey stirred from his chair. "I'll see you out."

He led Rex through the house, past a billiard room, and into a harlequin pattern marble-floored hallway in black and white, where a heavily carved oak staircase wrapped the walls and rose to what originally could have been a small minstrels' gallery.

"How can I reach you?" Rex asked at the front door. "Have the police returned your phone?"

"Not yet. I'm making do with a pre-pay." Trey read out the number, which Rex entered into his phone. "Are you going after Darrell?"

"I need to confirm where he is first."

"He has an agent in Manchester. I don't have a name, though."

"Thanks. I'll be in touch." Rex gave Trey a paternal clap on the shoulder.

As he approached his car, a call came in from Mike Fiske. Rex stopped on the gravel to better hear what the inspector was saying. Christopher Ells had been released on police bail. No snuff films had been found on his hard drive, and Timothy Holden, unwilling or unable to provide further information, had been allowed to leave the station the previous night.

"I had hoped to be able to make an announcement to the press today, but we don't have a solid enough case," the inspector said ruefully.

"I may have something."

"Well, don't keep me in suspense."

"I have a few more enquiries to make yet." Rex felt he had already stuck his neck out with his theory. He did not want to be caught with egg on his face if Darrell Brewster proved to have been in LA since Thursday. Before leaving the Old Rectory, he rang Helen to enlist her help.

As he drove back to Derby, Billy Joel's "Only the Good Die Young" floated over the airwaves, reminding him of the sentiment Helen had expressed on the opening night of the play after news of Cassie's death had come out. What a waste, Rex lamented. What a tragedy.

TWENTY-FOUR

By the time Rex arrived back at the house, Julie's red Spitfire was in the driveway, and he had no option but to park on the road.

"We're in the kitchen," Helen called out when he closed the front door behind him.

Circumventing the pile of cardboard boxes and holdalls, he went to join the women, who were seated at the table in front of their laptops and phones. "Hello, Julie," he said. "Did the school let you out early?"

"My last class ended at three and I came straight here. Sorry about the clobber in the hall. Helen put me straight to work on your case."

He looked enquiringly at his wife, who poured him a cup of tea from the pot. "I can see you've been busy," he said, surveying the evidence of their activity more closely. "Did you get anywhere?"

"We did." Helen took up a loose sheet of paper with her notes scrawled on it. "Darrell Brewster's casting agency is Mega Media Talent in Manchester. It didn't take long to find since there aren't many such agencies there. I said I was trying to locate Darrell and that I'd heard he might be in LA. The owner of the agency informed me, in his cheesy accent, that his client had not gone to LA, but had received some sad personal news and would not be available for a week or so for casting calls and bookings. I said it was to notify Darrell of his ex-girlfriend's death that I was trying to reach him, and I asked what had happened about LA. Cecil, I think he said his name was, told me he had emailed a taped audition to the studio and there had been some initial interest, but that Darrell had not been asked to fly out, or words to that effect."

"Nice work." Rex nodded with approval and lifted his cup of tea from the table. "I think we may actually be on to something."

"Julie has something for you too," Helen said, smiling at her friend.

Julie was today minimally made-up and wore a short-sleeved cashmere top and a light tweed skirt, in keeping with the teacher she was. "According to court records," she relayed, "Deborah Bradley, a previous ex-girlfriend of Darrell's, obtained a civil restraining order against him. This was two years ago, after she tried to end the relationship, and it's still in effect. I had to go through the process myself when I was being threatened by an abusive boyfriend."

Helen squeezed her friend's wrist in a consoling gesture.

"Thank you, Julie," Rex said. "That shows a pattern of behaviour. It seems Darrell Brewster doesn't handle rejection very well."

"I have his solicitor's name, if you want to speak to him," Julie said.

"Go on, then." Rex took out his notepad. Julie had done her homework.

"It's a Paul Reddit," she told him.

"Paul Reddit? He was in the play."

"Small world," said Helen.

"So it would seem." Often a coincidence spelt a clue. Rex drank down the rest of his tea and placed the empty cup in the sink. "I'll go and see if Mrs. Brewster is home yet. Perhaps she knows where her son is. First, though, Julie, do you need help bringing in the rest of your belongings?"

"I can manage, thanks. But before I forget, Jez Wyatt in my A-level class had rugby practice at the school on Sunday morning, and so couldn't have made that anonymous call on the other side of town. The coach told me. I'm meeting him for a drink later," she added nonchalantly, curling a strand of bleached hair around her forefinger.

Rex glanced over at Helen, who smiled back at him in amusement. "Right, I won't be long." He bent to kiss his wife and left the house.

Getting back in the car he had got out of just twenty minutes before, Rex drove to St. Swithins Close in Littleover for the second time that day.

Upon arriving, he immediately took note of the silver Vauxhall Hatchback parked on the paved apron outside the rectangular red-brick bungalow, and pulled up beside it. Tingling with anticipation, he pressed on the doorbell and knocked on the door for good measure.

A buxom woman with greying blonde hair drawn up in a poufy bun answered half a minute later.

"I'd like to speak with Darrell, if I may. Are you Mrs. Doreen Brewster?"

"He's not here. He went to California."

"If I could just have a minute of your time, in that case. It concerns Miss Cassie Chase."

He produced his card, which the woman took but did not read, instead casting a quick, wary glance over the area of off-street parking before standing back to let him inside the house.

"Please come through," she said, shuffling in her slippers into a living room which opened onto a dated fitted kitchen. An aroma of tinned tomato soup had strayed into the seating area.

Through a series of bi-folding doors, Rex could see a concrete patio and a square of patchy grass beyond, enclosed by a chain-link fence. Inside the sitting room, the magnolia-painted walls were covered with framed headshots of Darrell, running the gamut from preppy, in a white V-necked cricket jumper, to scruffy, his square-ish jaw sprouting four-day-old stubble. Rex detected a close resemblance between him and his mother in the regular features, although Mrs. Brewster's face was puffy, her eyes a washed-out blue.

She invited him to sit down on a sofa sheathed in a slip-on cover in a sheeny brown fabric. On a side table, next to a porcelain ashtray with scalloped edges, stood a black-and-white portrait photograph of a young officer in the greyish blue RAF uniform of World War Two, with similar facial characteristics to her own and—more remotely—Darrell's.

"Your father?" Rex asked, indicating the photo.

Doreen Brewster gave a slight nod and installed herself in an upholstered chair opposite him, the hem of her shapeless navy blue dress rising midway up swollen knees clad in opaque nylons.

"And what is your maiden name?"

"Hayes," she answered after a surprised pause. "What is it you've come to ask about Cassie?" She fidgeted with a stray thread from a front button, her hands riddled with varicose veins. Beside her wedding ring, Rex noticed a small dark sapphire surrounded by what he guessed to be paste diamonds, mounted on a slender gold band.

"I'm assuming you heard …?" he began.

"Yes. It's been all over the news."

"And your son is aware?"

"I sent him a text. Being in America, he hadn't heard."

"Did you know Cassie well?"

"I only met her a few times. Mostly Darrell went over to hers because her mother is unwell. Cassie didn't like leaving her on her own."

"It seems your son took the breakup with Cassie rather badly."

Doreen blinked a few times. "Well, he was upset. And he'd recently lost his father to a heart attack."

"I'm sorry. I didn't know. I apologize for having to ask, but I understand Darrell has a restraining order against him from a Miss Deborah Bradley?"

"That girl was unbalanced," Doreen stated, stiffening in her chair.

Rex rather thought it was her son who might be unbalanced.

"Are the police going to be coming round asking questions?" she asked.

"I can't speak for them. I'm following a private line of inquiry. Is Darrell your only son?"

"I have an older boy, Victor, who's an accountant." Mrs. Brewster pointed proudly to a colour photo on a table at the other end of the sofa, showing a young man with blonder hair than Darrell's and a more prominent nose.

Rex inched forward on the sofa and looked Doreen straight in the eye. "You're certain Darrell is in the States?"

"I drove him to the airport myself on Thursday morning."

"Where did you drop him off?"

"Outside the British Airways terminal."

"Did you see a ticket?"

"Mr. Reddit from the play bought him his ticket," she informed Rex with a defiant lift of the chin. "What are you suggesting? That he didn't get on a plane? He's contacted me several times from LA."

"Where is he staying?"

"With an old friend from an acting class."

Was she protecting her son or had she been duped along with everyone else? "Thank you, Mrs. Brewster, I won't take up more of your time." Her guard was up and Rex didn't feel she would give him more information, nor did he wish to appear to be harassing her.

She rose abruptly from her chair and escorted him back to the front door.

"Good day to you." Rex walked away from the bungalow and regained the Renault with deliberately measured steps, attempting to conceal his excitement.

Why would Darrell lie to his mother unless he had some terrible secret? It could not be he was simply embarrassed to admit that his hoped-for part had fallen through. Much as he felt sorry for Doreen

Brewster, Rex felt worse for Mrs. Chase. Doreen could always visit her son in prison.

He looked back and saw she was still standing in the doorway, staring after him. He waved before he got in the car and heard her slam the front door.

On the drive back to Barley Close, Rex reflected on the unusual nature of this case. Now that he had all but solved the whodunit portion, he needed to prove the how-dunit part, which would require the entire cast's participation; and the sooner the better.

First, he needed Inspector Fiske to grant him full access to the stage. To that end, he had to convince him that Darrell was a viable suspect, and told him over the phone everything he had collated.

"I may know how he managed to get onstage without anyone noticing, and this is the only way to find out," Rex concluded.

"Well, I'll be," Fiske said without finishing his sentence. "If you really think it's Darrell Brewster, we need to find him. I'll get my sergeant right on it. To tell you the truth, we were looking at Trey Atkins again and getting ready to bring him in for a polygraph."

"I think perhaps you don't give young Trey enough credit," Rex said. "He could have walked away when he discovered Cassie was being stalked and had a dependent mother, but instead he chose to support her."

"Young love. Doesn't it make you feel nostalgic?"

"Aye, well, unfortunately Darrell put an end to the happy future they had planned."

"I'm all ears to find out how."

Rex outlined his proposal.

"I'll see you shortly," Fiske said.

As Rex heard the click of the phone at the inspector's end, he knew he had not only stuck his neck out but had put it squarely on the block. Everything rested on the success of his plan. Next, he called Penny on her mobile number and asked if she was home.

"Not yet," she told him. "I'm in the car."

"Penny, I have a huge favour to ask of you. The last, I hope."

"Ask away. I have Bluetooth."

"I need you to call an emergency meeting of all the people involved in putting on the play on Friday night."

"When you say 'emergency'…?"

"I'd like everyone at the community centre by half past seven this evening. I've cleared it with Inspector Fiske. He'll be there."

"But why?"

"It's to prove a theory. I think Darrell Brewster murdered Cassie and I want to do a little re-enactment. I'm sure now he never went to LA." Rex could hear traffic in the background of Penny's phone as he waited for her response. "I'll get hold of Paul Reddit, Ron Wade, and Timothy Holden. And Trey. If you can convene the rest…" he urged.

"For seven thirty," Penny confirmed dubiously.

"I know it's a tall order, but I'm relying on your organizational skills."

"Flatterer. And what should I tell them?"

"That the inspector and I urgently require an hour or so of their time, and to bring reliable watches."

"Are the actors to wear their costumes?"

"Preferred, but not required. And don't forget Bill, Ben, and Tony."

"And myself, right?"

"Naturally. I plan to have a grand reveal."

"Sounds intriguing. I just hope they can all make it."

"Tell them it's for Cassie. We hope to bring her killer to justice before he absconds for good, and this just might be the clincher. But don't tell them who it is."

"Okay. I'll call you in an hour with an update. I'm turning into my street now."

Rex hung up and got to work at his end. There was no time to lose. Doreen would no doubt have tried to contact her son by now to tell him about the Scotsman's troubling visit to their home.

TWENTY-FIVE

"THANK YOU SO MUCH for coming at short notice." Rex addressed the actors gathered around him backstage. "I see that most of you are in costume or close to it, which lends verisimilitude to our re-enactment, and that you have all brought watches. Good. I don't want the distraction of mobiles, so if you could please mute them and place them on the tea table, Tony will keep an eye on them. Dennis, Rodney, and Andrew," he said to the three fictional detectives, "you will need to keep yours. I will be giving all of you your cues and directing the proceedings. Inspector Fiske and my wife are here as spectators."

"But we're not doing the whole first act, right?" asked Ben, who, along with his fellow stagehand, wore the stencilled tee-shirt, jeans, and trainers of Friday night.

"No, just the behind-the-scenes part that came after. Mr. Welsh, could you make sure the lights onstage are exactly as they were on opening night for the final scene of Act One, and flip on the projector." Bill hurried over to the back steps leading up to the stage. "Mr.

Holden, you have the lead role tonight, which is why I specifically requested that you wore your Father Brown costume."

A shyly pleased look overtook Timothy Holden's bland face.

"Only you won't be playing the *Timothy* Father Brown," Rex went on to explain. "You'll be playing the *Darrell* Father Brown."

"You what?" Holden said, blinking in confusion behind his glasses.

"He played you, and now you're going to play him."

"Darrell?" echoed several of the cast.

Rex surveyed the intent faces before him: Paul Reddit studious, his niece incredulous. Trey looked as though he were holding his breath. Ada watched with her mouth slightly open. Susan Richardson, in her stiff costume, but with her hair and makeup done naturally, stood with a hand on her chest, a stunned expression freezing her arresting features. Ben stared in curiosity. Dennis Caldwell, without his Poirot stage makeup, frowned with his half-grown eyebrows.

"I say," said Andrew Forsythe in his upper-crust voice. "This is a turn-up for the books, what? Still, so long as it's not one of us."

"Darrell Brewster?" Snyder, in his Sherlock tweeds, glanced over at Susan, apparently linking their names together. He turned back to Rex. "How?"

"That's what we're about to find out," Penny told him.

"You mean ee's not in LA?" Bill asked, re-joining the group.

"You finally twigged. Good lad," Ben teased his friend.

"A person says ee's going to America, I believe him. I hoped ee'd go to Hollywood and become famous, so we could all say we knew him back when."

"'Alas, poor Yorick, I knew him well,'" Snyder misquoted snidely.

"Thank you, Rodney, for the Shakespearean aside," Rex said, "but we're on the clock and I need you all to take your places. The shot was fired at seven forty-five, so let's synchronize our watches. It's now seven thirty-five. Ron, who is unable to join us due to a sales meeting, we'll just assume is in the car park getting his migraine pills. Tony, please take your seat at the table and work on your lesson plans."

The art teacher sat down and poured over some imaginary papers, his chin cupped in his right hand, a pencil in his left. Rex had not previously noticed he was left-handed. He turned back to the group.

"Could those of you who did not remain backstage after coming off the first act please take up position where you were on Friday at seven forty-five, as best you can remember; and from that moment proceed just as you did that night. We'll pretend that 'Timothy Father Brown' is with Miss Marple and Aunt Clara down the corridor. The three other male detectives, stay here. Mr. Ells, on the steps, if you please."

The butler in the play moved towards the stairs while Paul, Bobbi, and the stagehands followed Ada and Susan through the dressing room door.

Rex turned to Helen and Inspector Fiske. "The best vantage point is probably from this wall facing the back of the stage. Mr. Holden, I need you to come with me."

He led Timothy up the steps and alongside the stage, which was enshrouded in shadow, and asked him to hide behind one of the black panels close to the control button for the curtains, which had remained closed since the final performance. "Flat up against the wall, now, so I can't see you." Rex stood by the projector, as Bill had done on the opening night, and consulted his stopwatch. "Can you hear me, Mr. Holden?"

"Yes," replied a muted voice.

"Come out now and reach for the button, but don't push it, and then wait fifteen seconds, the time it would take for the curtains to close. I timed it from the DVD."

Father Brown emerged from his hiding place and put his hand to the button. Rex counted off the seconds on his stopwatch. "Now run onstage and stop in front of the chalk outline, and when you hear my stopwatch go off, pretend to shoot." The ring sounded. "This is where it gets tricky. Open the trap door and get down as quickly as you can, but watch you don't trip up." Rex re-set the stopwatch.

Father Brown pulled on the hook in the floor and wrenched open the door, and then scrambled down the ladder in his black cassock. Rex scooted down after him.

"Creep along the wall to the front of the trap room," he instructed. "Wait. Put on your priest hat in case someone spots you."

Holden pulled it from his garment. Rex followed his shadowy form in the dark, bowing his head to avoid the rafters. When he peered out of the trap room, he saw Dennis and Andrew on their phones looking up at the back of the stage, just as they would have been after the shot was fired. Rodney, his face likewise upturned and phone in hand, was standing at the foot of the steps talking to Ells, the butler, whose black trouser legs were visible further up, the rest of him hidden from view.

Tony got up from his chair at the table, strode to the dressing room door, and asked the person inside if they had seen Ben. Trey in his Henry Chalmers costume came out, and he and Tony dashed past the trap room towards the stairs. Rex heard the stampede of feet mounting the steps and running overhead. Ignoring Helen and Mike, who were watching the pantomime, he pushed Father Brown towards the dressing room door, which he closed noiselessly behind them.

"Into the end cubicle," he directed, hearing a commotion in the corridor. "Hurry! Close the curtain." The outer door opened to admit Aunt Clara and Miss Marple. "Assume I'm Timothy returning with you," he told them, ushering them into the storage area.

He closed the door on them and told Father Brown to exit the cubical. "Into the corridor. Go, go, go!" They both fled down the linoleum tile. "Open the emergency exit."

"Mr. Reddit's out there with Bobbi, Bill, and Ben," Holden informed him, peering through the glazed panel in the fire-escape door, which was propped open a fraction.

"Correct. So, where to now?"

Holden looked to his right. "Up the stairs?"

"Right you are."

Father Brown hitched up his cassock and hurried, huffing and puffing, up the staircase leading to the upper storey of the building. "How far?" he called down.

"Until you're out of sight. That's fine. Crouch down." Rex went to stand on a bottom step.

"How long for?" Holden gasped, his face, red with exertion, pressed between the wooden balusters.

"A few more minutes."

The fire-escape door opened from the outside and Paul Reddit, his niece, and the stagehands filed into the corridor.

"Seven fifty-three on the nose," Rex said approvingly, studying his stopwatch.

"The time I gave you," the solicitor said, walking towards the door to the dressing room, with the others behind him.

"The coast is clear," Rex called to Holden after the last of them had disappeared from view.

Father Brown traipsed clumsily down the stairs, holding up his hem in one hand while he held on to the bannister rail with the other.

"Time to hop on the bike," Rex told him. "Out you go."

"There is no bike," Holden replied, letting the heavy door swing back on its hinges onto Rex, who pushed it open again.

"There's no bike because Darrell took it." Rex stopped his watch at the birch tree. "Did your bike have a basket?"

"A wire one at the front." Holden expelled a loud breath. "I'm knackered!"

Rex smiled in sympathy. Darrell was younger and more agile, which would have shaved off several seconds from the last leg of his escape. No doubt he had got out of his cassock, having worn ordinary clothes beneath to make up some bulk, stowed the costume in the basket, and cycled across the grounds to the playing fields, where he had dropped one of the latex gloves he had worn for the crime. Inspector Fiske had not mentioned bicycle tracks, but by the time the police found the glove, it had rained.

"Right. Time to re-join the others." Rex put a friendly hand on Holden's shoulder and guided him back towards the building. "That was extremely helpful in that it proved it could be done." He held the fire-escape door open for him.

"By Darrell? But why'd he do it in the first place?"

"That, my friend, will become obvious in my summation."

The two men headed back to the storage area where the others were eagerly waiting.

TWENTY-SIX

"THANK YOU ALL FOR being so professional." Rex stood before the cast and crew with his back to the stage. "The reason behind choreographing your movements was to show how Darrell Brewster was able to pull off the shooting without anybody realizing he was ever here. How?" he asked rhetorically. "He arrives before five, dressed up as Father Brown in case anyone sees him, which someone does"—Rex turned to Penny—"and mistakes him for Timothy. He has the real gun concealed under his cassock, perhaps up his sleeve, and his large black hat pulled forward over his face. He waits for the main door to be unlocked and presumably enters the stage via the hall while Timothy is changing in the dressing room.

"Throughout the first act, he bides his time near the front of the stage behind the floating black panels until he hears the scrim for the attic scene roll down, the trap door open, and the projector click on. But then Bill hurries past where he's hiding, and Darrell realizes he's forgotten to close the curtains. He can't shoot Cassie from the wings and risk missing his target, nor can he step onstage in full view of the audience if he hopes to get away with it, and so, after waiting a few seconds for Bill to come back, he pushes the button himself. This accounts for the slight delay on opening night. He whips off his hat so his will be the last face Cassie ever sees on this earth, steps forward into the light cast by the projector, and, lifting the gun, aims for her heart. Cassie screams, as she is supposed to, but from real fear this time, and he fires. While the unsuspecting audience applauds, he opens the trap door, pulling it shut after him, and hides below while those backstage rush up the steps to investigate the loud bang.

"When the coast is clear, he sneaks into the dressing room, diving into a cubicle when Ada, Susan, and his double pass through. He goes into the corridor and hides at the top of the main stairs until the smokers among you re-enter the building, and then makes his escape before Ron returns last of all at seven fifty-five. By then, most of the spectators would have been back in the hall. I had Timothy act it all out to see if it was feasible."

Rex tapped his stopwatch. "The crime took less than ten minutes, from firing the gun to pedalling away to freedom on Timothy's bike. You could say luck was with the devil that night! But perhaps he never intended to get away with it. He may have been planning to shoot himself as well, but lost his nerve."

"But why?" Dennis Caldwell asked. "What motive could he possibly have had to kill Cassie of all people?"

"He was the jilted ex-boyfriend, vindictively jealous of Trey for winning Cassie's hand in marriage, and probably resentful, too, that his rival got the part of Henry Chalmers. I would not be surprised if one of the reasons he decided to shoot Cassie onstage was to sabotage Penny's play out of spite. And what's more dramatic than doing it in front of a theatre audience, especially if he intended to die along with her à la Romeo and Juliet?"

"I didn't know there had been something going on between Darrell and Cassie," Penny said in surprise.

"Nor I," added Tony, who was standing behind her with his hand on her shoulder.

"That was all over last year," Trey told them. "For Cassie, at any rate. We did our best to play down our relationship, knowing how he'd react. Obviously, we didn't know how far he would actually go."

"Of course not," Ada said in a consoling voice, rubbing his back.

Penny gave a helpless sigh. "Well, that explains a lot, doesn't it? He was waiting in the wings, figuratively and literally."

"And exit Lady Naomi for good," Forsythe chimed in, rather inappropriately, as Rex thought.

"How did you guess it was Darrell?" Penny asked Rex.

"Everything pointed to Father Brown, in retrospect. You saw a person whom you assumed to be Timothy in his costume walking towards the building earlier on Friday evening than you would have expected. Then Timothy's bike went missing. How could that be if he had arrived on foot? A pair of prop glasses were left behind in the dressing room, but Timothy wore his own glasses for the part. No doubt the imposter left them by mistake. Now, it had to be someone of similar height. Height is one thing that is not easy to disguise. All of you, with the exception of Timothy, Dennis, and Ada, are on the tall side. But those three had at least two people who could vouch for them at the time the shot was fired. Bill and Ben are of medium height. So, who was our phantom? It had to be someone who not only could pass himself off as Father Brown, but who knew the play backwards and where everybody would be at any given moment. You told me early on, Penny, that Timothy was a replacement, and as soon as you showed me Darrell's headshot, I thought he might fit the bill for our killer. But everyone thought he had gone to LA. When it transpired he was obsessed with Cassie, I felt it prudent to check. Furthermore, his grandfather had served in the RAF and might conceivably have owned a revolver like the one retrieved at the scene. Means, motive, and opportunity."

"Sherlock would be proud," Snyder remarked. "In fact, all five of our characters would," he added, indicating the four other fictitious detectives.

"Damn fine sleuthing," agreed Andrew Forsythe, applauding Rex, the antique cane hooked over his wrist.

Everyone joined in the ovation, and Rex felt well rewarded for his efforts. He held his hands out in appreciation and then raised them for silence. There were more revelations to come.

TWENTY-SEVEN

"DARRELL MADE THAT CALL, pretending to be me, to try to convince you Cassie had killed herself," Trey reminded Rex when the clapping had died down.

"Aye, I discovered his mother has a car matching the one described by the eyewitness at the petrol station. He must have known I was taking part in the investigation." Rex glanced over at Paul Reddit briefly and folded his arms. "Mrs. Brewster told me Darrell had lost his father recently, which I'm sure contributed to his state of mind. He must have thought he was losing everything, especially when his LA audition fell through. Whereas Trey, in his eyes, had everything."

"Including the lifestyle," Holden agreed. "The Beemer, the family house in the country, the prestigious job." He looked at Trey and shrugged in resignation. "You have it all, mate."

"Not Cassie," Trey replied bitterly, flexing his knuckles.

"Darrell Brewster is a selfish young man with a fragile ego, who had to be in the spotlight at any cost," pronounced Ada. "To think he was acting out his own role all along..."

"And played me for a fool," Susan said with stoic indignation.

"All of us," Trey amended.

Paul Reddit lifted his hands in a gesture of disbelief. "He said his agent was truly optimistic about his part on American TV. *Hur-rum*. Rex, do you really mean to say he fabricated all that as his alibi?"

"Up to a point. His talent agency informed my wife he ultimately lost the part and was still in England, but taking time off in the wake of Cassie's death."

"Bloody hypocrite," Ben swore in disgust.

"I lent him the money for his airfare," Reddit persisted. "He was confident he could pay me back. His prospects looked good."

"They're not looking good now." Rex was pleased Paul Reddit had brought up the matter of the loan of his own volition, but he had to wonder: did Paul like helping people in general or Darrell in particular? He recalled the conversation at the solicitor's office, where Paul had waxed sympathetic about gay rights. Of course, any romantic interest Paul had in Darrell might have gone unrequited. "You acted as Darrell's solicitor two years ago, did you not?"

Reddit cleared his throat in his customary way and cast a nervous look around his silently curious audience. "Yes. I already knew him from community theatre. We're a close-knit group here in Derby."

Rex refrained from commenting. "Did Mrs. Brewster call you after my visit to her house?" he asked with mounting suspicion.

"She wanted to let me know that she had told you about the loan for the ticket."

"Is that why you divulged just now that you had paid his airfare? Because you knew I knew about it? Are you by any chance harbouring a fugitive, Mr. Reddit?" Rex glanced over to Inspector Fiske, who acknowledged with a nod that he had taken note.

"Of course not!" countered the solicitor. "I thought, like everyone else, he was in LA."

Rex turned his attention to Reddit's niece. "Bobbi, you were friendly with Darrell. Any idea where he might have gone?"

"I don't. I'm sorry. We didn't hang out off the set."

"Most elucidating." Forsythe raised his cane off the floor, pointing it and missing Rex's nose by an inch. "But, much as we deplore his action, we must admire the fellow's steely nerve, what? To follow through with his dastardly plan and carry it all off in disguise! And almost get away with it!"

Christopher Ells, his ghoulish face expressing similar dark admiration, finally broke his silence. "Yeah, sorry mate," he said to Timothy Holden, "but that underbite … I bet you Darrell used rubber inserts in his jaw. And since he had to wear specs and a hat for Father Brown, it couldn't have been hard for him to pass himself off as you with a bit of extra padding." He closed his eyes and gave a groan of relief. "At least we're off the hook now."

Holden regarded him with disdain and said nothing. Clearly, he had not forgiven his friend for dropping him in it over the snuff films.

Inspector Fiske stood up from his chair in the back and joined Rex. "Persuasive as Mr. Graves' demonstration has been," he told everyone, "it remains a matter of conjecture as to whether Darrell Brewster is our man until we can find concrete evidence. I shall be seeking a warrant to search his home. In the meantime, I implore you all to keep this among yourselves. We don't want him fleeing these shores if he hasn't yet. He may well already know he's a person of interest. Thank you all." Fiske shook Rex's hand and said he would keep him apprised of developments.

"You not coming with us to the pub, inspector?" Ben asked. "We're all going."

Fiske smiled. "Duty calls."

"Rex, you coming to the Bells?"

Rex glanced over at Helen, still in her seat. She acquiesced with a nod. "Just one pint, then," he said gladly, in loving anticipation of a draft Guinness.

"Should we ring old Ron?" asked Bill. "Ee's probably out of his meeting by now."

"Nah," replied his fellow stagehand. "If he couldn't make it here, screw him."

Nobody objected. Trey said he couldn't make it either, since he had to pick up his mother at Manchester Airport.

"Some of us have to change first, so we'll meet you over there," Susan Richardson told Ben.

"Susan, just one minute." Rex took her arm and led her aside. "A mere loose end, but could you explain how blood came to be on the purple corduroys you were wearing on Friday?"

She looked up at him in shock. "How did you know about that? I cut myself on a tin of baked beans."

"Care to elaborate?"

Susan's eyes narrowed at him. "Well, if you must know, I was in bits when I got home on Friday night, not surprisingly. Rob was away on business as usual and the kids were being uncooperative. My youngest, who is quite old enough to fend for himself, was clamouring for baked beans on toast. I cut my thumb on the tin when I opened it. See here?" She thrust her right hand towards Rex, palm upwards, and he could make out a thin pink line, half an inch long, of healed flesh in the V of her thumb and forefinger.

"I held it under the cold tap and must have dried it on my trousers without thinking. I had to run a wash that night and threw them into the machine, only realizing they had a stain on them after I pulled them out of the dryer, otherwise I would have soaked them first. It wasn't that visible, but to me they were ruined, not to mention I would always associate them with Cassie's death. I decided to add them to the pile of donations I was getting ready for Oxfam."

"Which is where I found them."

"You were following me?" Susan Richardson's green eyes flashed at him in accusation.

"I assure you I wasn't. Helen is moving out of her house and had some items to give away. I came across your trousers purely by chance."

"And decided to have them tested for blood, no doubt," Susan finished for him. "You'll find that it's my blood, if the detergent didn't destroy all my DNA. And I gave you a perfectly reasonable explanation for it being there. You do think it's reasonable, don't you?"

"As reasonable a reason as I've ever heard," he agreed, which appeared to mollify her, for she smiled.

"I suppose I should just be grateful you were on hand to solve Cassie's murder." She made a move to follow the last of the actors into the dressing room. "We'll drink to you at the pub," she added over her shoulder. "See you there."

"Let's not jinx it," Rex replied. "We still have to find Darrell and get proof he did what I'm accusing him of. Are you not just a wee bit upset he might end up in prison?"

Susan turned around with a graceful shrug. "Not especially. Obviously, he was only paying attention to me to make Cassie jealous. I thought he was a bit immature, to tell the truth. I still find it hard to accept that he shot Cassie, but the way you laid it all out makes perfect sense."

Rex decided, out of delicacy, not to ask about her feelings for Trey. He crossed to where his wife was waiting and, holding out his hand, pulled her to her feet, and together they left the building.

"That was quite a performance you put on back there," Helen said as Rex drove them through the car park of the community centre. "Mike told me he was impressed."

"He's a very decent man, is Mike." Rex glanced across at her in the beam of car headlights passing on the road. "Not wanting to overstate my case, but don't you see certain parallels between Penny's play and Darrell's plan?"

"As in, Darrell picked up a few ideas from the plot? Yes. Penny's villain conceals his true identity and hides in the attic. Our villain disguises himself and lurks in the wings. Lady Naomi is stabbed, Cassie is shot, but in each case her privileged young fiancé is left to grieve for her. However, in *Peril at Pinegrove Hall*, it takes five sleuths to solve the murder, whereas in real life you did it all on your own!"

"Not entirely on my own," Rex countered.

Helen leaned into him, resting her head on his shoulder. "Anyway, what I really meant to say is that you are, without question, the big hero in all this. And my hero forever."

TWENTY-EIGHT

AT THE BELLS, BEN had explained that Darrell Brewster forwarded the digital recording of the dress rehearsal to him before allegedly catching his plane to the States, and the sound engineer had burned the audio-visual file to a DVD and given Penny a copy. Had Rex known who shot the video before Trey told him, he would have been on to Darrell sooner, but that was the nature of investigations; they rarely took the course of a straight line.

He fumbled with the key under the porch light and was just stepping through the front door with Helen when Trey called him in a panic.

"Speak up, lad, and slow down," Rex said in a calming tone of voice.

"He's here! Darrell, I mean. At Manchester Airport, Terminal Three. I spotted him a minute ago, checking in at the KLM desk for the next flight to Amsterdam. I'd dropped my sister off while I went to park, and the little ninny got lost. But it's as well she did, or I would never have seen him." Trey was talking a mile a minute, and Rex had put a finger to his mouth to motion to Helen not to make a sound as she followed him into the hall. "I sent Abby over to listen in at the desk," Trey went on explaining. "He has a one-way ticket. What should I do? I want to kill him!"

"Don't do anything rash, lad," Rex urged, concerned by the anger mounting in Trey's voice. "Let the police do their job and justice take its course."

"But he might get away! He took Cassie from me. I don't care what happens to me now." Trey's tone had become desperate.

"You still have your whole life ahead of you. You won't believe it now, but you will love again. I did. Trust me on this, Trey."

The young man said nothing for a moment, and Rex feared the worst. "Okay," Trey finally said, his voice thick with emotion.

"So just stand by," Rex instructed. "Keep eyes on him but don't let him see you. I'll alert Inspector Fiske."

"What about my mother? She's at Baggage Reclaim. She just flew in from Hong Kong."

"I'm sure she'll understand under the circumstances. I'll ring you as soon as I've spoken to Inspector Fiske. Stay put," Rex repeated firmly before he cut the connection to call the inspector.

Fiske answered immediately. "What's new, Rex?"

Rex told him.

"Amsterdam, eh? Well, you can get a cheap flight there. And most of them speak English in the Netherlands, if he's planning on staying there. But at this point, there's probably more panic than planning going on in Brewster's head. Right, then. I'll let you know when we nab him."

After an hour and a half of anxious pacing in the sitting room, during which time Helen managed to get him to eat a sandwich and drink a mug of strong coffee, Rex finally heard back from the inspector.

"We got Darrell Brewster, and in the nick of time. Airport Police arrested him at the gate about to board his flight. He had Cassie's mobile on him. We're taking him to Derby North. Should take us ninety minutes to get back there. Care to watch the interview, always assuming he doesn't cry for a lawyer?"

"Oh, I'll be there, never fear." Rex turned in elation to Helen after the call ended. "Mike is bringing him in."

"Good," she said from the sofa. "It was lucky Trey spotted him or he'd be over the Channel by now."

"I think I'll take advantage of Julie's absence to have a shower before I head to the station," Rex said. There was only the one bathroom.

Helen glanced at the mantelpiece clock. "She shouldn't be long, assuming she doesn't end up staying the night with Jeff. I do hope she doesn't go rushing into things."

"What's this coach like?"

"Younger," his wife stated.

Oh, dear, Rex thought, and headed up the stairs.

The shower felt relaxing on his tense shoulders, and he would have stayed under it longer had he not been worried about using up all the hot water. He dressed in a shirt, jeans, and pullover, and went back downstairs, where he found Helen watching a TV interview with Prime Minister Theresa May.

"Julie just called from her car," she told him.

Rex settled in beside his wife. "I'll wait until she gets here. I have bags of time yet, and I'll fill up the tank so we don't have to stop tomorrow on the way to Edinburgh."

Helen lowered the volume on the television and they chatted about the trip. A quarter of an hour later, they heard Julie enter the house.

"Hello, you two." She strutted into the sitting room in black suede ankle boots and a short skirt, and threw her handbag with abandon into an armchair. "Jeff is so fantastic! And dishy," she gloated. "And he has this really wicked sense of humour." She giggled at some remembered joke.

"Are you hungry?" Helen asked.

"We ate at the pub and talked for ages. And then we snogged in the car park, but I didn't let it go any further."

"Right, well, I'll leave you girls to it," Rex said, getting up from the sofa, wishing to be spared further details. "I'm off to the station. Inspector Fiske has made an arrest."

"Helen told me on the phone. Haven't we all had an interesting time tonight?"

Rex thought it might get a lot more interesting yet.

TWENTY-NINE

INSPECTOR FISKE SAT ACROSS from the suspect in an interview room. It was now past one in the morning. Darrell Brewster's left wrist was cuffed to the bar bolted on top of the table, his photogenic features blanched and drawn. DS Antonescu, an intimidating presence in his cobalt blue suit, had pulled his chair a short distance away. Rex watched and listened from the other side of the blind window.

"I want to speak to my mum before I say anything else," Darrell stated, with one hand zipping up his brown bomber jacket over a white tee-shirt. "Then I'll tell you everything."

Rex recognized the voice from the phone call, much as Darrell had managed to make himself sound like Trey.

"You're telling me you wish to confess?" Fiske asked.

Darrell bowed his dark blond head. His words came out muffled. "I meant to end it right there onstage, holding Cassie in my arms, but I couldn't go through with it. I thought of my mother, all alone now with my dad gone."

"So you left Cassie lying there on the floor after you shot her, and fled. Is that what you're saying?"

Darrell bit on his knuckles. "I wish I had died with her!"

"Now that you've been caught," Antonescu suggested.

"What was going through your head when you shot her?" Fiske questioned.

Darrell raised his face heavily, revealing a tortured expression. "I'd rehearsed what I was going to do over and over in my mind. Up until the moment I stepped onstage none of it seemed quite real. Then I saw the look on her face..." He shook his head in wondering despair. "There was nothing there but shock, and fear."

"What were you expecting?" Antonescu demanded.

"I don't know. Just... something." Darrell's light blue eyes held a glassy sheen as he gazed into the space between the detectives, presenting a three-quarter profile to Rex that underscored his straight nose and square jaw.

How far the lad would have gone in his acting career, Rex could only conjecture. Perhaps he would have remained a bit-part actor, as Cassie's aunt had categorized him. In any case, all his aspirations had come to this, and fifteen minutes of infamy would be as much celebrity as he would ever achieve. Rex pitied his browbeaten mother, who would finally hear the truth from Darrell's own lips after all the lies he had told her.

Inspector Fiske tilted himself back in his chair. "Did Cassie plead for her life?"

"No, she just screamed." Darrell frowned at the table. "It was ear-piercing. I couldn't hear myself think. I had to stop it." He started sobbing. "I'm so sorry, Cass! I didn't mean to. I loved you so much!"

His free arm slid onto the table, and his head fell into the crook of the leather sleeve, a shade dramatically, Rex thought.

The detectives exchanged almost imperceptible nods of triumph. When Darrell did not cease his whimpering, the inspector terminated the interrogation and switched off the black voice recorder.

He joined Rex in the adjacent room. "Looks like we've got our man. We'll let him talk to his mother and then take his full statement."

"Did you find the evidence you were looking for?"

Fiske smiled with satisfaction. "Like I said, he had Cassie's mobile on him when he was taken into custody at the airport, though he had ditched his own. Hundreds of text messages from him on Cassie's over the past weeks, not counting the thousands she must have deleted. They get increasingly desperate and threatening when she doesn't respond. He says he'll send for her in LA when he's settled, and they can seek their fame and fortune together. Next, he's suicidal and can't live without her, and lists various ways he's going to end it. Then he says he can't bear the thought of her with another man and won't let that happen. He loves her too much, and can't she see what she's doing to him, and so on. The last one was sent early on Thursday, saying he was about to board his plane for LA."

"Discovering she got engaged to Trey may well have been the impetus for murder."

"He would have discovered that when he stole her phone and read the texts between her and Trey. Even better: unspent bullets matching the one used in the shooting were found at his mum's house. If he had a second cartridge in the cylinder for himself, he had the presence of mind to take it out before leaving the gun beside his victim and making his escape. Mrs. Brewster said her father had left him the Webley in his will. Thanks for the tip regarding the photo, by the way. Flying Officer Bill Hayes was stationed at the RAF Radar Plotting Station on Lizard Point in Cornwall during World War Two."

"Indeed? And were you able to find the replica gun and Father Brown costume?"

"Not yet, nor the other glove, if that was his we found on the playing fields. And no sign of the bike."

"It may have been dumped in the environs of Morton's Petrol Station, where the anonymous call came from."

"We still have another place to search. He's been lying low these past few days at a mate's from the gym, known to us for selling steroids. May not turn up anything, but with any luck, we'll get DNA off the inner bridge of the glasses left in the dressing room cubical, which will further help put Darrell at the scene. It's unlikely he wiped them clean if he meant to take them with him, as I'm sure he did, since he was so meticulous in the rest of his planning."

Rex nodded in agreement. "It's often the case that the most cleverly planned murders are the easiest to solve, to paraphrase Raymond Chandler. It's hard not to slip up at least once. It's the random ones that usually elude us."

"Though it seems you have not been eluded yet," Mike Fiske said with his crooked smile. "Well, I owe you. Not sure we could have got there on our own, or at least as quickly."

"And I owe Paul Reddit an apology for suspecting him of harbouring Darrell." Rex realized he was going to miss some of the people from the theatre.

"Sticking around for the rest of the interview?"

"I think I know how it ends, and I need to get back to my wife. We're leaving for Edinburgh in the morning." Rex checked his watch. "Later this morning," he corrected himself.

"Well, if you're sure you don't want to share in the limelight," Fiske joked.

"I'm sure, but do me a favour, please? When you're ready to issue a press release, give Cindy Freeman at the *Derby Gazette* a heads-up, as my son in the States likes to say. She's the young reporter who approached us on opening night."

"A heads-up to give her a leg up?" Fiske asked with another smile. "Will do. She alibied Ron Wade, the producer. Saw him exit the community centre before the shot was fired. Your wife said you're off on your honeymoon at the end of the week. Cornwall, isn't it?"

"Aye, by some strange coincidence, since that's where our murder weapon saw military service. A colleague of mine is lending us his cottage for a fortnight. Helen will be glad of the break."

"They have murders down in Cornwall, you know. In fact, there have been some really grisly ones."

"Thanks, Mike," Rex said with an ironic smile of his own, adding, "I won't tell Helen you said that." He shook the inspector's hand warmly and promised to keep in touch.

ABOUT THE AUTHOR

Born in Bloomington, Indiana, and now living in Southwest Florida, C. S. Challinor was raised and educated in Scotland and England, and holds a joint honors degree from the University of Kent, Canterbury, England, as well as a diploma in Russian from the Pushkin Institute in Moscow. She is a member of the Authors Guild, New York. Her author website is www.rexgraves.com.